Praise for *The Fir*

'*The Fireflies of Autumn* is phenomenal. This is writing that is classical in its inspiration and its craft but also astonishing in the seductiveness and compelling uniqueness of its storytelling. I was so immersed in this book that I read it greedily, not wanting to leave San Ginese and return to the real world. There is immense beauty in this book, and there is great sadness and there is genuine tenderness. I can't recall when I was last thrilled by a book as I am by this one. Only one adjective will do: this is a great book.' —CHRISTOS TSIOLKAS

'I have never read a migrant tale so original, so breathtaking in scope, or so magical. I have not since stopped thinking about the characters in San Ginese.' —ALICE PUNG

'*The Fireflies of Autumn* reads like top-notch European literature, and Giovannoni's naturalistic prose and gentle irony is confident without being showy. Readers who are after a rich, rewarding experience will find themselves transformed by these earthy, rustic tales.'
—BOOKS+PUBLISHING

'Suddenly I was sitting on a chair in a cobblestone street in a small Tuscan village watching these captivating stories unfold. The writing is exquisite and the characters seemed uncannily familiar. This is the real Tuscany, in all its simple splendour and rawness.' —EDWINA JOHNSON, DIRECTOR, BYRON WRITERS FESTIVAL

THE FIREFLIES OF AUTUMN

Published by Black Inc.,
an imprint of Schwartz Publishing Pty Ltd
Level 1, 221 Drummond Street
Carlton VIC 3053, Australia
enquiries@blackincbooks.com
www.blackincbooks.com

9781863959940 (paperback)
9781743820544 (ebook)

 A catalogue record for this
book is available from the
National Library of Australia

Cover design by Mary Callahan
Map of San Ginese by Greg Ure
Text design and typesetting by Tristan Main
Author photo by David Patston

Printed in Australia by McPherson's Printing Group.

THE
FIREFLIES
OF
AUTUMN
and Other Tales of San Ginese

MORENO GIOVANNONI

Black Inc.

For Morena, Ugo and Ichlis
who were there

and for Antoni Jach,
another *fabbro*

Migrants never arrive at their destination

Contents

THE ENCHANTED GLADE
AND THE BABBLING BROOK

THE VISITOR

HUMAN SACRIFICE

SAN GINESE

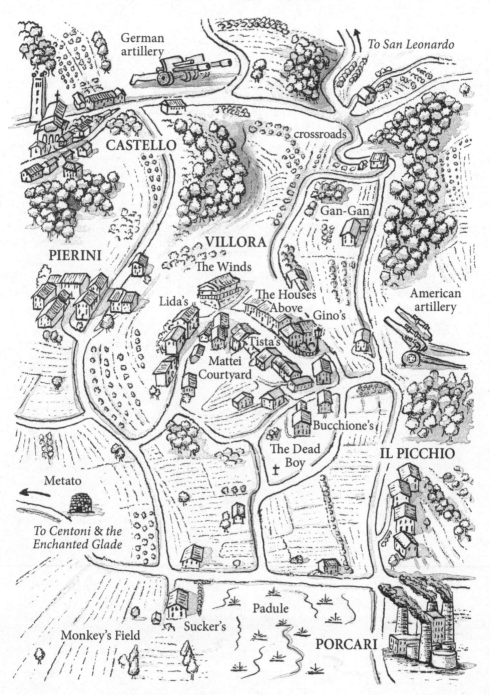

German artillery

To San Leonardo

CASTELLO

crossroads

Gan-Gan

VILLORA

PIERINI

The Winds

Lida's

The Houses
Above

Gino's

American
artillery

Tista's

Mattei
Courtyard

Bucchione's

The Dead
Boy

IL PICCHIO

Metato

To Centoni & the
Enchanted Glade

Padule

Monkey's Field

Sucker's

PORCARI

Ugo's Tale

Dear Reader,

When you leave your homeland, you leave behind the people you know, the people your mother and father knew, your grandfathers and grandmothers, brothers and sisters, cousins, uncles and aunts and neighbours, the people who know who you are immediately because you look like your father. You leave behind the courtyards, the roads, the lanes, the houses, the colours of the houses, the rows of houses, the names of small groups of houses, the shapes of the houses, the rooms in the houses, the stairs, the stones, the dreams that inhabit the stones, the fields, the walking paths, the irrigation ditches, the hills and the swamps, the grasses, the plants, the birds, the crops, the stables, the cows, the pigs, the rabbits, the chickens, the church, the belltower, the cemetery and the language you were born into, that is deep in your heart, and all the things that happened that anyone can remember.

Most importantly, you leave behind one thousand memories. You embark on a ship in Genoa and disembark on the other side of the world, and your life is a clean slate. You cling to a wife or a husband and to the children, if you have them already, or if you can you bring some into the world to fill the emptiness.

You abandon one thousand memories and you end up walking the streets of North Fitzroy, you, with your unusual name that no-one can pronounce, you, speaking a language no-one can understand.

What do you do with the memories you left behind and the need to tell the stories of your life and your ancestors' lives to your children? What if the only stories you have to tell are of people and places on the other side of the world? What if after a lifetime you still wonder whether you made a monumental, irreparable mistake by emigrating to Australia?

Normally the people you live with share the same memories and stories. So who can you share yours with, the stories that in the village of your birth are in the skin of the people and the memories that are in the stones?

I was born in Tuscany, in the province of Lucca, in a small village in the municipality of Capannori, named after its patron saint, San Ginese. Physically the area consists of small hills, all of which are well cultivated with vineyards and olive groves. It was paradise. While it is no longer so well looked after, it is much loved by the German and English visitors who have their summer homes there.

I was born on 20 December 1927. I left for Australia on 1 January 1957. Others of my family had emigrated before me: my grandfather and my father. Both emigrated to the United States of America, but both returned to Italy after some good fortune (that is, after making some money) and both died in Italy. A brother of mine emigrated to Australia but returned to Italy after just a few years and died there too. I have been back to Italy many times and while my father was alive he would always say to me: 'Why did all the others in the family who emigrated return to their native land to die and you refuse to?' My father was very sad that I would not follow in their footsteps.

I now want to go into some detail about what my father said of the day I was born. I was born at eleven o'clock at night. As you know, in those days women did not go to hospital to give birth. If all went well, they would give birth at home. They were assisted during labour by a woman who had some expertise in delivering children – a midwife.

An hour before I was born, there was a great storm that did not stop until two hours after my birth. My father used to say that because I was born on a stormy night I behaved differently to those who preceded me and that is why I would not return to San Ginese to die.

. . .

Some of these tales, dear reader, are set in the olden days, some in more recent times. All the tales are true. Most of them unfold in a hamlet of San Ginese called Villora. You may search for a map and images of this place and they will exist, but you will never find it. Just as migrants do not ever truly arrive at their destination, so those who remain behind disappear and become untraceable.

I have tried to write these tales to the best of my ability, but I am not a writer. Furthermore, some tales were recounted to me by others who had experienced directly the events described therein (sometimes with me as the protagonist), and some were given to me in written form, so I have simply reproduced them here with some minor changes. The tales are therefore told by many Italian voices.

Finally, although my Italian has deteriorated over the years, still I felt a strong desire to write in the language of my ancestors. I therefore sought out a translator expert in the writing of immigrants to translate my own work and the work presented to me by others into English. I entrusted to him a task that went beyond mere translation, and hope that you will find it satisfactory. I believe he was the right person for the work. Even now you are reading his words.

It is worth remarking that if these tales had not been written, the people in them and the events that befell them would have faded into boundless oblivion.

Ugo, age ninety years

THE BONES OF GENESIUS

The Percheron

Listen to me and I will tell you a story about the days when there was poverty in San Ginese and we used to go to America to work and make our fortune. I will try my best to tell it well, with the skilful use of words and some feeling from my heart.

At the age of twenty-four my father, Vitale, started working for the Madera Canyon Pine Company in California as a whistle punk. From whistle punk he was promoted to teamster. His favourite horse was a docile, intelligent giant of an animal, a French Percheron.

The Percheron waited patiently for the man to tell him when to start pulling, when to stop, when to back up. Vitale, who had been living at an Italian working men's hotel in Fresno before moving to the logging camp, spoke no English. He was lonely in California and missed his family and the life of the village, so the horse was a welcome companion.

Although there was good camaraderie among the men in the camp, and the team even included some Italians from north of Venice, near the Austrian border, who were expert timber-cutters and tree-fellers, Vitale was most at home with his loyal Percheron. He was what was known then as a proper Tuscan peasant and knew the proper Tuscan peasant's work. This meant he was used to working with animals,

in particular the cows back in the village that pulled the hay carts and ploughs and gave milk that was made into butter and cheese, and every year gave birth to a calf that could be sold. The stable near the back door of the kitchen at his father's house always housed one or two cows and their calves.

Now that he was responsible for looking after a horse – feeding it, grooming it, making sure it was strong and healthy and happy and ready to pull the log, stop or back up – Vitale was proud. He was the whistle punk when he first started, as this was the work they gave to young or inexperienced men, and he was proud of his promotion to teamster. In San Ginese only rich people owned horses, and looking after this horse made him feel rich.

He was happy that he could at least feel rich, as his American adventure had not been as successful as he had hoped it would be. In seven years he had earned a living but had not made his fortune. That would come soon, but he did not know it yet. He intended to return to San Ginese when the time was right and marry. Marriage too would come, but in the pine forest that day he was reflecting on his bad luck and felt disappointment and frustration.

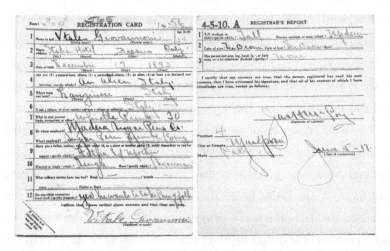

The day before the incident, government officials visited the logging camp and asked him and the other men a lot of questions. The officials completed a registration card with all his details. They asked him whether he claimed exemption from the military draft, and he said yes he did claim it. He did not want to join the army because he wanted to look after his mother and father (or 'folks', as the American official wrote on the draft card). This was not the only time they had come looking for him, and he was always worried that they were going to conscript him. He managed to lie low, and on a few occasions when he felt it would be safer to hide, he hid. Even his employers helped to hide him, so that after the war he was able to return to San Ginese without serving in the army of the United States of America.

As he was reflecting on his poor American luck, he was also troubled by this official visit. Thoughts of bad luck and ominous officialdom chased each other through his head and gave him no rest the night before the incident.

On that day the Percheron was reluctant to follow the man's instructions. He sensed the man was distracted. The Percheron waited to be acknowledged, for his presence to be appreciated. Just a word, a friendly tap on the shoulder. He could not work unless he sensed a partnership between himself and the man. Then he realised that not only was the man distracted but that he was too. He could no longer read the signals coming from the man. He didn't know whether he was being asked to pull or stop or back up. Having failed to establish the working rapport, he tried very hard to continue without it, but kept getting it wrong. And yet they had worked together for several months now. The horse loved the man and responded well to him: he sensed that the man was an experienced handler of draft animals, although the horse didn't think of himself in those terms exactly. He thought of himself as himself.

Vitale knew that the only way to work with a horse was to use a psychological approach, because a man's strength cannot match that of a horse. He tried to anticipate the horse's behaviour and gently encouraged responses consistent with the needs of the work. So what happened that day was a shock to both the man and the horse. Vitale was surprised to learn that he was capable of such a thing, he who in his later life – as he grew to be very old – would have a reputation in the village and the surrounding district for his gentleness of manner and whose son would tell stories to his grandchildren about their gentle grandfather. When the village spoke about him decades later, mention was also made of his father, Tista, from whom the mild manners were inherited, and how the gentle nature was in the blood of the family.

Vitale spoke to the horse and tugged and tapped him in the usual way, and the Percheron did not move. Vitale called out again, louder, and shook the reins. The horse tried to back up.

Vitale lost his temper and picked up a tree branch from the floor of the pine forest and struck the horse on the side of the head.

Now, the eyesight of horses is designed for grazing and looking out for danger at the same time, but horses adjust their range of vision by lowering and raising their head. They are also a little colourblind. In the pine forest, the Percheron could see the green of the trees but not the browns and greys of the carpet of pine needles, could see the blue of the sky but not the white of the clouds. In what is therefore a landscape resembling a drab mosaic, objects that are motionless convey very little information to a horse. Nor can horses see things nearer than three feet directly in front of them without moving their heads.

The Percheron did not see the blow coming, although the man was quite close to him.

Who knows what it was? Maybe his mind was churning over the bad luck, the government officials, their questions, the war. Perhaps it was his true secret nature that, tired of being buried under the gentleness and kindness that was his trademark, for once in his life ripped its way out of his guts and into the freedom at last of the warm June air.

The horse quickly reared up and away from the blow, tossed his head and screamed, pawed at the ground. The scream of a horse may sometimes be referred to as a whinny or a neigh, but these words may disguise the horror a horse can feel. A horse can indeed scream, and it is a horrible thing to hear.

Hidden in the screams was a frantic wish for the pain to stop and a prayer that it would go away, and panic at a world that had turned upside down in an instant. The man was a stranger suddenly and a monster.

The eyeball had popped out of its socket and was split. The horse was blind in one eye.

Vitale pulled hard and held the leather reins tight to prevent the horse from bolting. He struggled with his friend the horse and spoke to him reassuringly. He was finally acknowledging the horse's presence. He hid his disgust at his own violence as well as he could. When the horse had calmed down and was crying in silence and Vitale was exhausted, not only physically but also in his emotions, and barely keeping a grip on the reins, he removed his shirt and wrapped it around the horse's head and over the frightening eye. He took water from the drinking bucket and soaked the improvised bandage, hoping the cool would soothe the pain.

With the horse's screams, some of the other men came running. Vitale understood the enormity of what he had done. He told the boss that the horse had walked into a low-hanging branch and had poked his eye out and that he had done his best to calm him down. See how he had bandaged the head? The gentle man accompanied the Percheron back to the camp in silence, one hand stroking the thick, powerful neck.

The precise details of the Percheron's fate after this are not known, as Vitale did not remain with the Madera Canyon Pine Company much longer. Soon after, he left the logging camp and continued working in the vineyards around Fresno, where after several rich grape harvests he made his fortune and returned to San Ginese.

I was a small boy when my father, Vitale, told me this story, and I cried all night at the thought of the large, innocent, blind horse. My father later added a brief epilogue, which was that the horse continued to work with one good eye. When I became a man and reflected on this I wondered whether the addition to the story was true or whether my father had made it up. I also wondered why my father would tell me the story of the Percheron, and decided that it was because the truth is sometimes necessary, especially to a gentle man seeking absolution.

After I had been in Australia for sixty years and my father was long dead, I myself having reached the age at which he died, the time came when all that was left for me was to reflect on certain events in my life. It was then that I understood why sometimes at night, in the silence of the old house, my father, Vitale, the gentle man who lived to be eighty-nine and whom everybody in San Ginese loved, remembered the Percheron and wept.

The Bones of Genesius

The bones of Genesius, which is the English name for Ginese, lie in an ossuary under the war memorial next to the church. This is the oldest cemetery in living memory, apart from the forgotten cemetery underneath the houses of Villora. The New Cemetery is past the church, down the hill, and next to the other one they have built, the Newest Cemetery. The demand for burial earth continues to grow.

...

The peasant grew all manner of crops. Agriculture was of the mixed variety: grapes, olives, wheat, corn, beans, hay, milk, cows, beef cattle, working cattle, pigs, chickens, rabbits. The work never ended.

In Winter the peasant in San Ginese spent his time fixing the vines – pruning them when they were made pliable by the moist air and tying them up, the latter according to the *filagna* system, so that they would be ready for the growth that came in Spring.

The peasant farmers grew the salix, a genus of willow tree, in rows around the borders of their fields next to the drainage ditches, and coppiced them, meaning they cut them back regularly to stimulate the growth of young shoots, which they harvested to tie the vines and use as kindling to light fires in their houses. The thicker, sturdier stakes grown from the salix, the *calocchie*, were used to prop up the vines. Strong *agagio* poles were used at each end of a line of grape vines to hold up the entire row. The poles were burnt at the tip so the charcoal would stop the pole rotting after it was driven into the ground. They would last three or four years, five if you were lucky.

Vineyards were sprayed with fungicides, a practice dating back to the times of Tista. Copper sulphate was sprayed on the vines weekly in Spring, and again after rain, to prevent fungi and moulds attacking the plants.

The earth was sliced and broken up with a shovel, and then turned over in preparation for the planting of new vines. The deeper the soil was dug, the better it retained the moisture when it rained.

The peasant picked olives in November and December and sent them to the communal *frantoio* to be crushed for oil.

In Winter firewood was prepared for the following Winter. This gave the green wood time to dry out so it would burn easily.

In Spring the soil in established vineyards was tilled. Leguminous plants that had been sown between the rows of vines – lupins, wild peas and broad beans – were dug into the soil for nitrogen.

All kinds of vegetables were sown in Spring, both for domestic consumption and for selling to contracted buyers and cooperatives. These included corn (for example, the May corn known as *maggese*), tomatoes and potatoes. Corn was harvested in Autumn.

At Spring's end, and in early Summer, hay was cut and left in the fields to air and dry for a few days before being piled high onto hay carts pulled by one or two cows and stored in lofts above the stables so it could be tossed down easily into the mangers from which the cows ate.

Cows were milked all year round. A wealthier peasant typically kept between four and six cows and one or two calves in the stable next to the house.

...

Although excrement is often thought to be present at the end of things, in fact it is there at the beginning too. From excrement (which, if liquefied, is poured over the earth, or if mixed with straw is dug into it) grow corn and grapes, onions and potatoes, carrots and long stringy green beans.

With this in mind, there is one important feature of that collection of hamlets known as San Ginese that it is well to note and useful to remember, from the very beginning. And that is this: for the entire year, and particularly in Summer, the village and the surrounding countryside are impregnated with the smell of excrement: human, cow, rabbit, chicken and pig. A sickly sweet gas brews in small subterranean cisterns from whence it wafts into the village street and courtyards. It is also released in the fields when the villagers spread the fermented brown liquid, which they call *perugino*, over growing crops. Visitors gag and flee from Villora, the village on the dark side of the San Ginese hill. Meanwhile the *perugino* from the other hamlets, clinging to the side of the San Ginese Hill, also seeps into the swampy land below the village, slowly.

In the life of the village, shit and piss are such staples that there are two sayings to describe someone who is an arsehole (which of course is where the shit comes from). The first is *ti manca il manico e sei un getto* (all you need is a handle and you'd be a shit-bucket), and the second is *sei colmanio* – an abbreviated form of *sei con il manico*, although this longer form is never used (you've got a handle, implying that you've already got a handle so you *are* a shit-bucket).

But this is by the by.

One final thing to consider on this matter is that the consequences of excrement can be problematic, as you probably know. From excrement comes methane, and from methane come cataclysms.

...

The time came when the village was saturated. The miasma had crept into the spaces between the stones and the bricks, filled the spidery hairline cracks and fissures in the mortar and in the tiles on the roofs, as well as the broken concrete underfoot, got into the soil for metres below ground, was trapped in subterranean air pockets, squeezed into the substratum, clawed its way past the bedrock and was absorbed into the water table, easing its way down down down to the centre of the earth. It gathered in corners of stables, filled the emptiness between the straws of hay in haystacks, the spaces under roofs, occupied attics, and rose up to the eaves and collected under them. The gas rested under cloths draped over bread baskets, between rounds of cheese on shelves, inside barrels of salted meat, it wrapped itself around the washing hanging on clotheslines, wafted into empty ovens and sat there, slid into ice-chests through gaps in the lids and waited, and in the last week breezed into the cavities in the red-brick communal bread-baking oven.

The villagers noticed nothing. They were accustomed to the hydrogen sulphide gas produced by decomposing human and animal waste – sweet manure – but could not detect the methane, which was odourless. They noticed nothing even when it happened, it was so quick. Some were asleep, others had just awoken and were feeding their cows and pigs; no-one was off to the fields yet.

The Tomato, *Il Pomodoro*, a short round man with pale yellow skin, so named because he was anything but the colour of a tomato, rolled over onto his side and became aware that his wife was shuffling about in the kitchen downstairs. He heard the noise of pots and pans being handled, sensed her absence from the bed, shifted his foot across to feel her warmth and check that she was really gone, and gathered the courage to make the effort of muscle, bone and cartilage required of his stomach, spine and hips to sit up on the edge of the bed, followed by more stomach, spine, hips and then knees, to stand up. But before he stood he sat, trying to remember something, something. His cigar was on the stone floor against the wall, where he'd placed it the night before after one last wet suck-and-swallow of nicotine saliva. He leaned over and picked it up, fumbling for it twice before wrapping the middle and index fingers and thumb of his right hand around it and shoving it into the corner of his mouth and under his tongue. He was looking forward to hot coffee, and milk poured over stale bread with sugar sprinkled on top so it formed little mounds. His cellar was filling with gas even as he stumbled down the scalloped stairs, worn by two hundred years of feet.

The village and an area out to a radius of one and a half kilometres was replete. Through some accident of physics and chemistry, the last place into which the gas poured was Pomodoro's cellar.

And here comes the overflow now, up the steps and through the trapdoor and into the kitchen. And there's Pomodoro, delicately placing kindling in the stove and striking a match on the cast-iron top.

The village exploded in the direction of the sky. The stomach of the earth heaved, the skin of the earth flapped, a tablecloth shaken flicked the cluster of houses towards Heaven, who opened her welcoming arms. There went Bucchione's house, Lilì's house, Erica and Claudio's houses and the other twenty-six in the village, as well as thirty-two stables and outhouses and everything else. For a moment they were whole and sitting on the ground, and then they were twenty metres in the air, still intact, and then they disintegrated.

Bricks, stones, mortar, chunks of concrete, twisted steel rods, mercurial pools of molten metal, pieces of rafter, shattered terracotta tiles, fragments of flagstones, shards of glass: wave after wave rocketed towards Paradise, closer and closer to where God was. Into orbit it all went. The legendary stone from Gino's garden wall spearheaded the upward thrust of debris and dust, closely followed by a brown tidal wave of liquid manure, a giant fountain of shit. The row of *le case di sopra*, the Houses Above, followed after.

The earth broke three metres from the church and the separated mass was sucked down and slipped away in a landslide. The church, with its adjacent ossuary, was left perched on the edge. Looking crazed but still standing, it leaned, adjusted and settled.

Meanwhile in Heaven, inside the clouds, the wind was spinning wet particles of dust into clusters. As the particles became heavy with moisture and the clusters started falling, they gathered more water until they were delivered to the earth as raindrops.

If you go to San Ginese, even now you will hear the people talk about the *piovuti* (those who fall like rain from the sky), which is the name they give to all newcomers.

The Imbeciles and the Fig Tree

or, And They Lived Happy and Content

In Villora, one of the hamlets in the village of San Ginese, there lived an old woman called Ancilla, with her two nieces, Liduina and Mariella. They were the poorest family in the village as they had no fields, no men to do the hard work and only one scrawny cow, which they kept in the stable of their amicable neighbour Bulletta. They also had three scabby, unfeathered hens, a small worm-infested vegetable garden about four metres by four metres in area, and a *bruciotto* fig tree, which is the Florentine variety. Their neighbours gave them soup and bread, sometimes, and distant family members from Colognora came to visit once a year and always brought them three large wooden tubs of salted pork.

They lived in the row of crumbling clay-brick houses in which Tommaso Giovannoni, the killer, also lived, the row known as the Houses Above. This was across the street from Tista's house, where Tista lived with his wife, son Vitale, daughter-in-law Irma and their children, Ugo, Sucker and Lida.

Tista's family were the witnesses to everything that happened to Liduina and Mariella.

Tista's wife was also called Ancilla, and every Sunday morning after Mass, Ancilla from one side of the road took the poor Ancilla on the other side a bowl of bean soup or a bit of pork or some lard or a few slices of *farinata*, which is polenta made with vegetables.

Because they were poor, the three women were often starving, although they disguised it well. As is the way with starvation, it can be difficult to identify after one has reached a certain stage of hunger and physical decrepitude, especially if, as they did, you wear several layers of clothes. Another consequence of poverty is that your excrement is on public display. Because they did not have their own privy, every morning Liduina and Mariella could be seen carrying three chamber-pots to the common cesspit to empty them. And as if to remind them of the misery of their lives, 'Nibale, who lived nearby and who enjoyed reminding everyone of the fleeting nature of life, was always walking past and chanting:

> *Dura, dura, non durerai*
> *L'appetito non manca mai.*

It was as if he was the only one who knew that all good things in life passed and that new desires replaced old ones. While you were caught up in everyday matters, your life was trickling away, and sooner or later you would be brought back to reality. Or at least that was what we thought it meant because, to tell the truth, the saying didn't make sense. Nevertheless, it sounded like a gloomy philosophy, and he made sure he told you in case you'd forgotten or had never known.

> *Dura, dura, non durerai*
> *L'appetito non manca mai.*

...

Liduina and Mariella were both imbeciles, having been born that way. Liduina was born first and, when her parents saw her – the shape of her head and her eyes and the positioning of her lips, from which a little drool flowed – they decided they would produce another child quickly to make up for the mistake of the first. However, in the throes of the act that generated the second child, the father in his imagination saw a perfect image of the first, and when he looked up at the bedstead, under the rosary and crucifix on the bedroom wall, a small fiend, crouching on its haunches, smiled at him.

It was unusual for two children in the same family to be born deficient, but that's just the way it was. People didn't know what to make of it, except to say the things people say in these cases, which is to question the moral character of the mother and the father and to reflect on the punishments that God inflicts on sinners, nodding wisely as they did so. The girls shared a squat physique – plump, almost round in their first few years – and had the physical attributes that are usually found with imbeciles, such as widely spaced eyes and drooping eyelids and lips, although they smiled easily and were generally good-humoured and friendly, so that you wanted to pat them on the head as they stared cheerfully up at you. Their mother and father, on the other hand, were tall and upright in bearing, the father handsome and the mother stunningly attractive.

Their mother, who resembled the Virgin Mary of the painting inside the church sacristy, was a dark beauty, with an oval face, a high forehead, large green eyes and long black glossy tresses that swept around her shoulders and down to her hips. She had a habit of winking with her left eyelid, especially at the men, who didn't know if it was a nervous tic or if she was teasing them. If you walked past her after she had washed her hair you could smell the freshness of the soap and the light dose of vinegar she had run through it. It was after her bath that men appeared from behind buildings and left their stables to wander aimlessly in her vicinity. All of them, and some of the women too, wanted to wrap themselves in her hair entirely. By contrast, her daughters' hair, which was kept short so it could be easily cared for, was a pale brown colour and looked and felt like rope.

She painted her lips bright red every day of the year, not just on feast days, and touched up a beauty spot on her left cheek with a small piece of coal from the fireplace. Her poor handsome husband knew what the people of the village said about why she had given birth to two such unfortunate creatures. Her daughters, however, loved their mother beyond human understanding, as children do, and marvelled at her beauty, believing that one day they would grow to be as beautiful as her.

Apart from being a beautiful woman, she was also impatient. When the municipal workers came every year with their horse-drawn wagons to spread a layer of crushed rock over the single road that ran through the village, she complained of the dust. She'd be out in the street after they had passed through, cursing them, waving her arms, thrusting her hips forward, driving the men mad with desire. Then when it rained she complained of the mud. Now, of course, everyone liked to grumble about the state of the road, which, mind you, would have been worse without the crushed rock, but the way the girls' mother complained made it obvious that she was going to do something about it. She spoke with such confidence and in such a strong, loud voice they could not help but think that one day she would.

In fact, she did. After much arguing and persuasion and granting of special favours in the conjugal bed, she finally convinced her husband they should emigrate to America, as many from San Ginese had done.

It was perfectly normal that they should want to sail over to New York and perhaps catch the train to California or Chicago, where many Sanginesini had gone, so no-one thought twice about it. They would leave the girls, who were then five and six years old, with her sister, Ancilla.

Ancilla had never attracted a suitable suitor in her youth and, after seeing her younger sister's first child born and feeling an outpouring of love for the unfortunate child, had decided to dedicate her life to spinsterhood. She would care for her sister's family, especially the little girl, whom she loved as she would any creature of God. God in His infinite wisdom had made Liduina as she was, and who was Ancilla to question God's will? Her resolve only strengthened amid the despair that followed the tragic birth of Mariella, when the old maid truly embraced her unmarried fate and lifted the burden of the two imbeciles onto her shoulders, where she carried it for as long as she lived.

By the way, God's wisdom is always 'infinite', or it was in those days, and it became such a strong habit for people to think it that people say this even now.

...

Entrusting their daughters to the care of their maternal aunt, the mother and father had left for America many years ago and had not been heard from since. It was said later that they fled to leave behind the two imbeciles they had brought into the world, and that even if at first they had intended to return, they soon abandoned the thought.

From time to time someone coming back from the new world brought news about the mother and father of the imbeciles, about how they were prospering and had produced healthy children. When these recent arrivals spoke, they made sure they could not be heard by the three unfortunate souls who had been forsaken, but the news always reached Ancilla, Liduina and Mariella.

Their normal state of despair deepened each time this happened and, for the daughters, was accompanied by a sense of shame that they had been abandoned because they were unworthy. Of course America, which was a rich and magical land full of beautiful things, was not for people like them. Their shame sat heavy in their chests, pushed against their foreheads from inside their skulls and gave them headaches. It ate their stomachs and made them look at the ground as they walked. It was only the love of their aunt, the old maid Ancilla, that stopped them from putting an end to their misery. Such thoughts are uncommon among imbeciles; nevertheless, they sometimes occur.

By secretly listening in on the whispered conversations of the returned, they overheard that they had two brothers in America. They imagined they must be healthy, handsome boys and were overjoyed and made plans for when they would all be together one day. But time passed and there was never any news from their mother and father.

...

In a small coop they kept three unhappy hens that, because of the general gloom of the proprietors, and because they had few scraps to eat, only laid one egg a day between them. So every third day Ancilla, Liduina or Mariella ate an egg. They also had a goose tied by one of its legs to the fig tree to guard it. The two girls, who loved reading, and Ancilla, who taught them tirelessly, knew that a flock of geese had saved Rome from an invasion, so one goose would have no trouble saving a single tree.

Their father had bought the cow before leaving. He scraped together enough money by selling their only field, calling in every small favour he was owed and begging some distant relatives for help, and even stole the money in the poor box at the church up on the hill at Castello, a final paternal gesture to assuage his guilt before abandoning his daughters. It was a plump cow at first, but had become thin as time passed and it had little to eat. With the cow's milk they made just a small quantity of butter and cheese. Because they had no pasture, all they could do to feed her was graze her along the side of the road for a few hours each day.

One of the girls, usually Liduina, who was the oldest, walked her slowly to Centoni or Lecci or Il Porto and back. They would head off in the morning as the sun was coming up. The cow waddled and the girl waddled, both with their eyes downcast, the latter intent on guarding the former, reluctantly greeting people along the way.

'*Ehi, Liduina. Come sta la zia Ancilla?*'

And she would grumble a bit under her breath because the passer-by was interfering with her supervision of the cow. 'My aunt is well. Leave me alone, I have to mind the cow.'

The cow would stop, swing her tail backwards and forwards and sideways down her flanks to shoo away the flies, and Liduina would wait patiently for her to tear a few mouthfuls of grass from the verge, take a few steps forward and pause again. From time to time the cow suddenly spread her back legs apart a little, raised her tail and released a flood of piss on the ground. Other times she would shit. Out it came in wet clumps, forming a neat round pat of concentric rings of semi-liquid grass onto the ground. On later excursions, Liduina would collect the cowpats after the sun had dried them and throw them in a sack she carried over a shoulder to add to the pile they used to fuel the fire at night.

Liduina was impatient with the cow. She believed the cow was cunning and trying to cheat her by not eating enough. She thought that all the cow wanted to do was sleep on her feet. 'You'd better eat, cow,' she would say. 'We need milk. It's no good you just standing there in the sun half asleep, chasing flies with your tail. Eat some grass.'

Liduina believed it was her responsibility to make sure the cow ate enough so that there would be milk every evening.

...

Ancilla's deceased mother and father, the grandparents of the two girls, along with every other person in the village, had taught her (and her beautiful sister) about the value of a cow. The children absorbed the village teaching about cows in their blood and in their bones. The lesson also found its way deep into their hearts and stayed there. Ancilla had passed it onto the girls when their father bought the cow.

People watched as cows were hitched to carts, watched cows pulling empty carts to the fields and hauling them back piled high with hay, potatoes, corn or firewood. People heard the lugubrious sounds of the cows as they waited for their mangers to be filled for the evening feed. Pitchforks rained hay down from the lofts in the stables. The sound the cows made was deep and mournful and full of anticipation. They were silent when their udders were caressed and tugged for milk, and they grieved when their children were taken from them. Cows by nature were generous, and in return were cherished and never sold, especially by the poor.

The villagers saw Liduina walking her cow and knew what it meant to her and her sister and her aunt. Everyone knew without thinking. They nodded instinctively even as Liduina scolded them for interrupting her supervision of the grazing cow.

...

Of course, apart from the cow, their most valuable possession was the fig, a large, robust, healthy tree with a wide crown, which grew in front of their house in a small raised bed with a low stone wall around it. It was forbidden to sit on the wall, and the two sisters and their aunt gave chase to anyone who came near their exceptional tree, which for three months every year produced dozens and dozens of baskets of fruit. The figs were the dark-skinned kind, with bright red flesh that was plump and sweet, and the tree was renowned throughout the district for its abundant crop and its lengthy fruiting season. They were proud of it and kept it close in their hearts as the one source of hope in their lives.

They wasted not a fig. If one fell to the ground, they would jump on it immediately, wash it and add it to their store. They made jam. They sold jam. They ran lengths of string through a dozen figs and hung hundreds of these strings on the outside wall of the house in the sun, bringing in the dried figs every night. They sold them at the market.

They watered the fig tree assiduously, carrying buckets every day to the village fountain and back, all through the spring and even in the blistering heat of summer (into which the fruiting season often extended). They quenched the miraculous tree's thirst, pouring water over the hard ground and keeping the roots damp and cool. They fed it the miserable chicken droppings their miserable chickens made. They guarded it against thieving boys and other passers-by.

Mariella and Liduina took turns sleeping on the floor just inside the front door, which was left ajar, a few metres from the tree. They threw rocks at the boys and anyone else who tried to steal their figs. The goose made its loud honking sound at would-be thieves.

They wanted the fig tree to be healthy and strong for the day their mother and father returned from America, so they could show them they had cared for it, as they had been taught, and were worthy of their parents' love. On this day their shame would be lifted from their shoulders.

...

Ancilla became sick during the tenth winter of their abandonment. After she had been bled using leeches and cupped by the local witch, her fever had not diminished, and they needed money to pay the doctor and to buy medicine, which, in the days before penicillin, almost never cured you. The girls decided they would sell the cow, over the protestations of Ancilla, who was prepared to die rather than agree to this. She knew that it meant the end. The end of a family's prospects, the end of hope. A cow gave you milk, cheese, butter and more, if you were lucky enough to get it to calf. They were poor, and the poor never sold their cow.

Despite their imbecility, the two girls were good at commercial affairs and, ignoring Ancilla's protests, they sold the cow, paid for the doctor and paid for the medicine. The aunt nevertheless died.

The death of Ancilla was such a tragedy in the lives of Liduina and Mariella that there was no possible comprehension of it. Their loss transported them entirely beyond measurable pain. It was a blow to the heart that was repeated every morning when they awoke. From that moment they lived their lives in a stupor known to them alone.

Without the cow and their aunt, life was unbearable for the two sisters, and the fig tree became even more important.

Ancilla died in the winter, and the following spring it seemed the tree would be late in fruiting.

32

...

During Mass on the third Sunday in Lent, the priest told a story from the life of Jesus. In this story Jesus curses a fig tree that has never produced any fruit, causing it to wither and die. Without their aunt, who always explained everything to them, Liduina and Mariella, who were seated in a corner at the back of the church, gasped, buried their heads in each other's arms and sobbed quietly. Spring had arrived and their tree had not yet produced any fruit, just like Jesus' fig.

As soon as Mass had finished, they shuffled quickly out of the church, holding hands, and hurried down the hill to Villora. People saw them and laughed at the two imbeciles whose short, ungainly bodies, horribly thin under their clothes, swayed as they ran, their arms flapping about wildly.

Mariella searched the dust on the ground around the fig tree for Jesus' footprints. Liduina examined the trunk for marks. She imagined that if Jesus had cursed the tree he would have touched the trunk and charred it.

Yet they could not remember anyone who resembled Jesus approaching their tree in the daytime. And at night they had slept with the door open, and their sleep had not been disturbed by a tall man with a brown beard and a long white robe near the fig. Nor had the goose caused a ruckus.

When they visited the priest's housekeeper to ask her about the significance of the story of the fig tree, the ignorant woman told them it meant that sooner or later God punished the wicked. Liduina and Mariella did not feel they had done anything wicked, except that they were born imbeciles and had been abandoned by their parents. All they could think of was that because their parents had left them they must be wicked. So God would now punish them by killing their fig tree. After their aunt had died. After they had sold the cow.

The housekeeper told everyone about her visitors, and very soon the news got around. And so we all knew what was going on in the minds of the two imbecile sisters.

That spring, the figs did not come. The sisters continued to water the tree, which seemed to ignore their entreaties and reject their love, just as their mother had rejected their love all those years ago and had gone away to America.

They believed that God, and even Jesus directly, had cursed not only their tree but them as well.

Mostly, for the rest of that spring, and the summer, and then the autumn, they sat on the stone wall under the tree, eating less and less of the little that their neighbours and distant relatives could spare – one egg, a bit of salted pork or lard, some soup every few days. They killed and ate their three chickens and finally even the goose. Their small vegetable patch was invaded by voracious worms that ate all their *cavolo nero*, including the roots.

And all that the neighbours – Ancilla across the road, and the other neighbours, Tista and Vitale and Irma and even Tommaso – could do was watch. By the time the winter came around again and the entire village was experiencing hardship and no-one could spare any food, or wood for the fire, Liduina and Mariella had stopped hoping Jesus would return to lift the curse.

The Angel of Sadness draped its wings over the village and slept.

The two imbecile sisters were stunned by the cold and the hunger and the deep disappointment of their lives – their imbecility, the disappearance across the ocean of their beautiful mother and their handsome father, the death of their aunt, the loss of their cow and their chickens and their goose, the devastation of their garden and the sterility of their fig tree – and they sat, they sat, holding each other by the hand, just inside the door of their freezing, crumbling, clay-brick house, looking out, sat, guarding their tree, sat, waiting for spring, sat, waiting for the fig to produce fruit, sat, their eyes large and round and sunken in their sockets, sat, their lips thin and the skin stretched with hunger across their cheeks, sat together, sat, waiting.

Tista and the Mute

Tista was the first to leave. He went to America in the days when its streets were paved with gold and Lady Liberty newly towered over the entrance to the bay of New York, that ample basin into which almost four hundred years earlier another Tuscan had sailed: his Florentine countryman, Giovanni da Verrazzano.

At Ellis Island, after passing the medical examination in the large hall, he walked down the stairs at the New Jersey end and turned

right into the railroad station vestibule, where he bought a ticket to California. Some years later his son Vitale underwent the same scrutiny – a doctor waiting at the top of the stairs listened for shortness of breath, a possible sign of pulmonary tuberculosis, and inspected his eyes, teeth and throat. Vitale then descended the same stairs and bought the same ticket.

After sailing to America from Genoa in 1902 on the S.S. *Lahn*, an express mail steamer of the Norddeutscher Lloyd line, Tista worked in the vineyards around San Francisco and taught the Americans to make wine. He lived at first in the same Italian working-men's hotel in Fresno where one day Vitale and his neighbour Tommaso would also stay. In fact, on the day Vitale arrived there, the hotel owner pointed to a bunk in the corner and said: 'Vitale, this is where your countryman Tommaso slept before you.'

...

From the moment he returned, they called Tista an *americano*. They called anyone in the village who went away and came back an *americano*, even if they had been to Canada or Argentina (where Julio the Orphan went), Venezuela or Australia.

Tista came back and married Ancilla, the maidservant. Hers was a good name for a young woman and a popular one for a nun in those days, though she did not observe the vow of chastity, bearing him three children and quite enjoying the making of them and the rehearsals for those that were never made. Though it was considered unseemly to make a big show of such matters, everyone in the surrounding houses could hear her triumphant exclamations and his profoundly earnest grunts through the thick stone walls, as the couple went about producing Vitale and his two sisters.

Ancilla was a local girl, born just one hundred metres from the house where she would later live with her husband. Upon marriage to Tista she did the normal thing and moved into his family home.

In the old photographs Tista is a funny man with a moustache who some say resembles the Tramp in Charlie Chaplin films. Tista's wife Ancilla was tall. They said Tista was gentle because of his shortness, and that he was conscious, from the moment he grew into self-awareness, that just as Fate had made him short, Fate could also deal him any other hand it chose, after which there was nothing left but resignation to Fate. In a village that revered Tallness, Shortness taught him Humility as a foil to Humiliation.

By the time he was a man and his mother and father had died, Tista's reputation for profound piety and good works had spread throughout the district. Pilgrims knew that if they came down the side alley into the *Aia dei Mattei* (the Mattei Courtyard) and knocked on his back door there would be bean soup with a small piece of pork sausage and bread to eat, and clean straw and blankets for sleeping near the cow and her calf in the warm stable next to the kitchen.

Tista's two daughters married and moved to their husband's houses, while his son Vitale also did the normal thing and brought his wife home. It was shameful to go to the wife's house. So everything was as it should be.

When Tista and Ancilla were old, the daily programme of the family included Bible readings and an evening rosary, which was dutifully observed by the other occupiers of the house: their son Vitale (who was short and gentle, like Tista), Vitale's wife, Irma (a tall, hard, hard-drinking woman who brought Tallness to the family's blood), and their children, Lida (who would first lose her first-born son and later be widowed and after that become a living saint, as women who had suffered did in those days); Bruno, the Sucker of the Flat Thumb

39

(known as Sucker for the habit of sucking his right thumb); and Little Ugo, the youngest and the sweetest of the grandchildren, upon whom Tista and Ancilla doted.

With regard to Sucker, it cannot be left unsaid that even as a mature man, when questioned about his flat thumb, he, Sucker (who had sucked it hard from birth and therefore flattened it), would proudly display this deformed digit, curling his other fingers into the palm of his hand and thrusting the thing right up into the questioner's face for a close look, while smiling his white even-teeth smile under his neat thick brush of permanently waved hair, which at night he gathered and preserved in a hairnet.

...

It was Tista who went to America first, thus starting the tradition of going away. His father, Genesius, had borrowed money to buy land

and had not been able to repay the debt, so his son's purpose was to work and make money to liquidate the loan, which he did.

After he returned, Tista told stories about his time in California – especially about the different people he had met. The Chinese, for example. *'Le mani delle persone cinesi sono come le nostre,'* he would say. 'The hands of the Chinese are like ours.'

He was always glad he had seen the world. He did not want to be the toad who was born in a hedge, lived his life in that hedge and died in the same hedge. One thing he had learnt in America, however, was this: in San Ginese you were just whoever you were; in America you were always someone else.

He also maintained that a man should avoid a fist fight at all costs. If you are dealing with shit, he would say, get a shovel and keep it at arm's length. Why would you want to approach it and get your hands dirty?

When Tista left for America, Vitale was nine years old, and it was nine years before he saw his father again. Soon after Tista returned, Vitale left and was away for ten years, including the period of the Great War.

In those days a worker in the city earned less than ten thousand lire in a year. Vitale returned from America with fifty thousand, which he deposited in the bank and collected interest on every six months. He bought two new cows, three new fields (including ten thousand square metres situated between Pasquale's house and Il Picchio, in low-lying land that had its own spring, next to the stream that served as the communal laundry) and a horse and carriage, richly fitted out with a fine harness and accessories for Sunday outings. Other than this he lived modestly in the old paternal home with his wife and children and parents. He could, however, afford to send his family to the seaside for a month every summer, and supported the family of Leonide, his widowed sister.

As they had with Tista, locals and those from neighbouring villages knocked on Vitale's door, asking for handouts and loans. They knocked again when they came to make repayments. In the end, by the time the last round of borrowers knocked to repay their borrowings, the currency was worth a fraction of its original value. This was after the great economic disaster that struck the world, and San Ginese too. Money that once could buy you a fertile field was now barely enough to pay for a chicken, so when Vitale's son Ugo decided to marry Morena the family's resources were greatly diminished.

Meanwhile there was an older sister, an older brother and a younger one too, born eighteen years after Ugo, all of whom needed to be supported by Vitale's cows, pigs and fields. The late-born brother, Irmo, the Young One, placed an additional and unexpected economic burden on the family. The fortune made by Vitale, and before him Tista, was gone, although the family lacked for nothing.

...

Tista owned the longest, widest, most abundant overcoat on God's dear earth, and Little Ugo hid under it whenever he was afraid of the world (in truth, no matter what anyone might say, there is no other fear than that, the fear of the wide world). Under his grandfather's overcoat the boy was warm and safe and happy. It could not be said then, let alone now, which of these three qualities – warmth, safety and happiness – took precedence over the other. This was especially the case in the middle of winter, when Tista would walk with him up the hill in the bitter cold of night to the church for the Christmas Novena. As the word *novena* suggests, they did this on nine consecutive occasions. Seated on the aisle in the first pew, Ugo would disappear under his grandfather's greatcoat and into the musty old man's smell, which was sweet to him.

It was one such Novena night, after Tista and the boy had returned home, and as he lay on his corn husk–stuffed mattress in the gloomy below-stair nook where he slept, that Ugo understood the enormity of what his father, Vitale, had told him earlier in the day. In the dark a screaming horse with a frightful eyeball dangling from a bloodied socket, hanging from the optic nerve, galloped towards him, and Ugo flew up the stairs to the bedroom of his grandparents, Tista and Ancilla, and buried himself under the blankets in the warm space between them. Here again he gladly inhaled the odour of old people, stale perspiration sweetened by age and love and the occasional exhalation of gas gently trumpeted from their ancient guts and trapped under the bedclothes. Fortunately the old saying was correct: farts and dreams stay under the blankets. So when he awoke in the morning, all was well.

Vitale was a father with a cool heart – not a cold heart, but a cool heart – and Ugo preferred to spend his time with Tista and Ancilla. He followed his grandfather everywhere: to the stable, to the vegetable garden and to the cellar (which the old man still commanded, as his son had not turned out to be a good winemaker). If Ugo misbehaved, Tista gently slapped him on the head with his soft felt hat. Ugo was admonished once for taking Tista's shoehorn, which was made from a real cow *corno*.

Ancilla would send him on errands to the vegetable garden to pick a few carrots or some silverbeet, a sprig of rosemary or some parsley. In exchange he was allowed to taste the food on the stove or in the cauldron over the fire before anyone else.

It was to Tista and Ancilla that Ugo turned when his legs ached at night, from above the kneecap down the front, along the shin, an ache that required Sloan's Liniment, which Tista and Vitale had brought back from America and which could also be bought in Lucca if there was any money in the house. Tista patiently rubbed Ugo's legs for half an hour, and the warmth of the balm and the massage breached his flesh and penetrated his bones until the pain dissolved and he slept.

He was surprised every time when he awoke in the morning, alone in their bed. Where had they gone? He would jump out from under the blankets and step over to the window that looked out onto the courtyard to see if they were down there, sweeping, feeding the animals or doing other old people's work.

...

One day a pilgrim arrived in the Mattei Courtyard. It was the custom in those days for the devout, who were usually those without work or land to till, to wander the country roads claiming they were on a pilgrimage to some holy site, such as the cathedral that housed the Holy Face of Jesus in Lucca.

This particular pilgrim, who was mute, made it understood that he was seeking work and a place to stay, and Tista took him in and gave him regular meals and a place to sleep in the stable in exchange for his labour.

The mute also worked for others in the village and occasionally slept in other stables. In time he became the village mute. It was good for a village to have one in those days, as it was to have a hunchback, for luck.

Speaking of hunchbacks, there was one from Pontedera who came every September to the *fiera* at Colle, one of the biggest fairs in the district. At this fair, fires were built and grates set over them for roasting chestnuts and a pig. While the hunchback's companion played a small accordion, the man with the misshapen back told a story. Little Ugo would always ask Vitale to take him.

'Please … please *papà*, take me. Let's go, *papà!*'

But Vitale was too busy, so Tista would take him. They would walk one hour to get there and one hour to get back.

As the hunchback recited his rhyming tale, which was usually about a delinquent priest or an innocent virgin, to the accompaniment of the accordion, a third member of the small carnival troupe walked around the crowd, collecting coins and selling horticultural guides based on the phases of the moon, which were printed in colour on small squares of paper.

The hunchback later settled in Colle and brought the hamlet much good fortune for many years to come. People hoped the mute in San Ginese would turn out to be as auspicious a presence as his misshapen counterpart in Colle.

· · ·

The mute had been living with Tista and his family for six months when one day he started talking. It was such a surprise that when people heard about it they did not believe it. Many villagers visited Tista's house and poked their heads through the door at dinnertime to hear for themselves. Some said his voice was not like what they thought it would have been if he had been able to talk, while others said he had precisely the voice they imagined he would have had if he had been able to talk. Tommaso said the mute's voice was deeper than he thought it would be. There was much confusion about whether he could be said to have had a voice when he was mute while others wondered whether he could still be called 'the mute', so the discussion was dropped and they just listened and engaged him in conversation so they could hear and marvel at his voice.

Everyone was amazed at how he had managed to keep quiet all that time.

Most people decided he had done it to elicit pity and find a warm welcome. Someone got it into his head that what the mute had committed was a kind of fraud, that he had obtained food and shelter under false pretences. Tista defended the man, arguing he had always earned his food and pile of fresh straw. As to why a man wished to be mute, who were they to judge his motives? In any case, he may have been suffering from an illness or he may have been the victim of an evil eye. When they asked the mute, he said that he had lost the ability to speak after receiving a blow to the head from a cow.

Despite Tista's best efforts, the mute was reported to the *carabinieri* and taken away for questioning, whereupon the judicial authorities charged him with having no fixed abode and lacking identity papers, which were not really serious charges. The roads were full of pilgrims with nowhere permanent to live and, anyway, who had an identity card?

Tista appeared at the hearing before the magistrate and spoke in favour of the mute, praising his hard work, punctuality and modest habits. Tista's reputation carried such weight that the court dismissed the charge and scolded the person who had reported the mute to the authorities. The mute decided to continue his pilgrimage and left soon after, thanking Tista and all those who had been good to him. Unfortunately he did not settle in the village, which consequently missed out on the good luck he would have attracted.

. . .

Tista died in his bed in his son's house (which had been his house once), surrounded by Vitale and Irma and his grandchildren. He was the second male head of the family to die in that house, after Genesius. Tista was seventy-five years old and had been in bed for a year. It was the summer of 1942 and Vitale was working at the Metato near his olive grove, spraying copper sulphate on the grapevines. Ugo's aunt Leonide told him to run to get his father because Tista wasn't well. Ugo was fifteen years old and as he stood at the foot of Tista's bed, the old man said: 'Ugo, *muoio*. I'm dying.' And he did.

Tommaso the Killer

At the start everyone insisted that although Tommaso Giovannoni had the same surname as almost everyone else in San Ginese, he was not related to them. There were no murderers in their family, they would say. Later, everyone would proudly point to their family relationship with Tommaso the Killer.

Anyway, here's the story.

Tommaso Giovannoni and Folaino Dal Porto were the best of friends. They went to America, worked together on a ranch in California and made a lot of money. One day when Tommaso went into the town for some business, the boss rancher handed over their year's earnings to Folaino to be split between the two of them. Folaino up and left, taking it all with him to Canada. The news slowly made its way back to San Ginese.

Seven years later and within three months of each other they returned to San Ginese. Folaino arrived first, and always denied that he and Tommaso had had a falling out. '*Vaffanculo, pezzo di merda!*' he would say to whoever asked him. The matter always seemed to get him more excited than it should have if there had been no truth to the rumours.

Everyone remembers the day Tommaso returned to San Ginese. His two sisters were waiting for him in front of the house, wearing their good

Sunday dresses, although it was a Tuesday. Giorgio della Rana, riding his horse back from the market, had seen him walking along the road from Lucca, detoured to San Ginese and knocked on their door mid-morning to tell them Tommaso was on his way. He had ridden past him at Pieve San Paolo, so it would probably be another hour before he got home.

His sisters had been expecting him after receiving his letter. They said Tommaso had caught the train across America from San Francisco, and when he got to New York he wrote to say he was disembarking at Genoa in about a month. Some people wondered what he was going to do in New York all that time, given that a transatlantic crossing took less than a week. Ugo's cousin Gino said Tommaso was probably hanging around Manhattan going to whorehouses. As we found out later, he wasn't visiting houses of ill repute. He was buying a gun.

Soon after Giorgio's visit the whole village knew that Tommaso was back and on his way to San Ginese and a possible confrontation with Folaino. A kind of relay system was set up to monitor Tommaso's progress. Sandrino the postmaster at Castello had the only telephone in the district, so when the postmaster at Carraia rang him and told him that Tommaso was just then walking past, Sandrino sent his son Federico quickly down the hill to Villora to tell the sisters where their brother was.

Pretty soon all the surrounding villages heard the news of Tommaso's walk. It seemed to precede him, on horseback and in handwritten notes gripped in grubby hands by small children who were told to run, or ride bicycles, to tell so and so that Tommaso, the enemy of Folaino, was on his way.

When Folaino was given the news by Michelino, the son of the local butcher, who had been told by Federico, who had ridden his bicycle to Il Porto after visiting the sisters, Folaino stood just inside his door and called Tommaso a *figlio di puttana* (son of a whore), loudly proclaimed that he was innocent of any wrongdoing, said Tommaso could get fucked (*lo mando affanculo*) and that there was no money owed to anyone and he could stick it up his arse (*se lo ficchi nel culo*), and so on.

Folaino prefaced his outburst against Tommaso with another outburst, calling Our Lady a whore too (*puttana la Madonna*), and God a dog (*Dio cane*). This was quite common in these parts, and no-one really meant anything by it, but if Tommaso had heard him speaking like that he would undoubtedly have laid into him. Tommaso had a horror of that kind of language.

When the first villagers saw him, he was walking along the bottom of the long San Ginese hill in bright sunshine. Soon a crowd was lining the road in silence. A flock of sparrows flew overhead and performed acrobatics, and a cow mooed at its calf in a stable next to the dairy cooperative.

In about twenty minutes Tommaso would be at the crossroads. To get to Il Porto, where Folaino lived, he would have to keep walking straight, passing the turn-off, which was on the right. Everybody was waiting to see what he would do.

There was talk that he and Folaino had fought, not over money, but over a woman or a horse. It was even suggested that Tommaso had made inappropriate advances to Folaino and been rejected. Whatever the reason, it was accepted that Tommaso bore a mighty grudge and felt justified in exacting his revenge.

What form this might take was also the subject of much speculation. Someone said that in California Tommaso had become an expert knife wielder, having worked on a big ranch where he castrated thousands of calves. Some were certain this was what he intended to do to Folaino. Others who had seen too many Tom Mix movies at the Palazzo Cinematografico in San Leonardo believed he carried a six-gun inside his belt under his collarless peasant shirt, and indeed you could see people peering at him from a safe distance to see if he was carrying any concealed weapon.

The crowd grew. Women who were sweeping, spreading corn out to dry in the sun, shelling peas and hanging out their flaxen bedsheets, which flapped gently like pale gold sails in the wind, left their courtyards and made their way to the roadside. Men dropped their scythes or tethered their working cows and ran to join the women.

Only the occasional '*Salve, Tommà!*' and '*Bentornato, Tommà!*' broke the silence. 'Hello! Welcome back!'

Everyone was thinking about the horrible fate that awaited Folaino. Tommaso was known to be a deeply religious man, quiet and hard-working. Religion can make some people kind and forgiving. They're the ones who read the New Testament. Tommaso was one of those who only read the Old Testament, believed in an eye for an eye and was hard and unforgiving, like you can imagine Abraham was, who was prepared to slit his own son's throat.

As he approached the turn, Tommaso would either continue straight towards Il Porto and a fateful meeting with Folaino or he would turn sharp right, towards Villora and his little house in *le case di sopra*, the row of houses opposite Vitale's place.

Tommaso turned right and headed home. There was a collective gasp and a murmur among the watchers that turned into a sigh and faded away. It was the sound of disappointment.

That more or less ended that.

He strode into Villora a lonely figure, wearing a sad grey hat, carrying a dilapidated brown suitcase, almost as though he'd never been to America. To greet him, his sisters left their doorstep, which they hardly ever did, as if the threshold were an invisible wall beyond which lay danger. It would not have surprised anyone if Tommaso had told them to stay inside until he got back from the other side of the world. They were church-going spinsters who took up the collection during Mass and were always arranging flowers for the church altar.

Tommaso was back and life in the village continued as usual. As he had done before he went away, he waited for his neighbour Irma to milk the cow in the late afternoon, and when he heard the dull dong of full milk cans he would cross the street with his little aluminium saucepan and come down the side alley to the courtyard.

Clacaclac. You could hear him coming in his wooden clogs as the sun went down. He would hand Irma a penny for a little milk for the next day's breakfast and *clacaclac* his way back home. We even started calling him Clacaclac. Here comes Clacaclac, people would say.

On the Saturday after the Tuesday of his arrival, Tommaso walked out of his house and turned right. His fields, his cellar and his stable were to the left. The church was that way too, as was the village bar. But he turned right. That was the way to Il Porto and Folaino.

If you had been looking out for him, you would have seen him from the steps built into the roots of the old fig tree on the path that led down into the vegetable patch at the back of Vitale and Irma's house. He would have disappeared and then reappeared from behind Julio's stable, heading towards the drained swamp. The clacaclac sound of his wooden clogs carried clearly across the fields.

At the crossroads this time, he turned towards Il Porto. By the time he was at the Metato, the bend in the road named for the chestnut kiln, all of Villora knew where he was going. This time there was no doubt.

The men and women out in the fields dropped their shovels and hoes and pitchforks and followed at a safe distance, so that by the time Tommaso reached the bend in the road at Il Porto he had quite a following.

Folaino was at the side of the house, squatting near the hutch and skinning a rabbit. He looked quite ordinary, even undignified, for a man who had made a lot of money in America.

'Dal Porto Folaino! Scoundrel! It's me, Giovannoni Tommaso,' boomed the voice. He would have made a good Abraham, or even God of the Old Testament.

Folaino came out from behind the house, holding the skinning knife, and hesitated when he saw Tommaso and the crowd of onlookers. Then he clenched his jaw around a bad set of teeth, as if he'd made up his mind to fight, stepped over to the gate, which was chained and padlocked, and stood there defiantly. He gripped the handle of the knife so tightly that the knuckles of his right hand were white.

'Away from my property or I call the police!'

'I have come to advise you that at the moment I have no need of the money you stole from me. But I am not a rich man and eventually I will need it. Until that time you can keep it. However, one day I will return to ask you for it – with the interest!'

'I don't owe you anything, *figlio di puttana! Son of a whore.'* With every imprecation that he uttered – and there were many others, referring to God's Mother and God himself – Folaino shook a menacing fist and spat through the bars at Tommaso, who did not even bother to wipe himself clean.

At Folaino's blasphemy the crowd saw Tommaso's eyes open wide with horror and his face set with determination. Everyone had come expecting at least a punch-up, if not a fight with knives, and maybe some blood, but Tommaso swivelled around and headed back where he had come from. *Clacaclac.*

'*Vigliacco!* Coward!' Folaino called out. 'Go to hell, you and those sluts of your sisters!'

54

Most people were satisfied. It had been quite a good altercation, although some in the crowd wanted more. People mumbled about Tommaso being all talk and no action, promising much and not delivering. Tommaso went home and everyone else returned to their work.

For a while the village waited for something else to happen, but nothing did. Like many other men who had been to America, Folaino had bought new fields and more cows, and deposited what was left in the bank in Lucca. He was able to dress all eight of his children elegantly, educate them at the Jesuit school and the convent, make large donations to the church and generally saunter about San Ginese as if he owned the place.

Meanwhile Tommaso continued to work his fields, leading a miserable existence, just him and his little aluminium saucepan.

...

Ten years after Folaino returned from America, his only daughter, Mariuccia, married Nedo del Carlaccio and came to live in Villora. Folaino bought a horse and carriage for two, with a driver's seat as well, and on the wedding day paraded his virgin daughter through all the hamlets of San Ginese, taking the long way round up to the church so that everybody could get a good look at her and her virginity. The rest of the family followed in three motorcars, which were rarely seen in these parts, driven by groomsmen in fancy dress, as if this were an American film.

After the ceremony the couple repeated the tour in their bright new trap, all polished wood and brass, this time as the bells of San Ginese tolled on the hilltop. Folaino made a generous donation to the church that day and the bells rang for one whole hour, the time it took for Mariuccia and Nedo to visit the villages and arrive at the Baracca tavern for the wedding feast.

People wondered how Tommaso might have felt about this public display of wealth and fertile abundance from Folaino, but on the day of the wedding Tommaso was nowhere to be seen. Of course, no-one expected to see him, then or at any other time. He kept to himself and went out of his way not to be seen.

He had slipped once when walking home with a full saucepan, and the milk made a white arc in the air and landed on his head. He was left sitting on his backside in the street, embarrassed but unhurt. Folaino, who had just turned the corner in his car, slowed and stopped to watch, with the engine running.

For a few years the story of Tommaso's two walks would be mentioned in conversation in local bars and courtyards, when the heat of summer had exhausted everyone and the only energy most had left was reserved for sitting in the shade on low, grey stone walls, listening to the stories told by the more energetic. The speaker always made sure Tommaso was not present before starting.

The story often included reflections on the different forms of luck that accompanied you if you left for America in search of your fortune. Some people noted how those who returned hardly ever had children, as if on their return God punished them for having left the place where they were born. Of course this wasn't true of Folaino, who had produced all his children before he left.

Then Tommaso's story died and was buried and nobody could be bothered digging it up to tell anymore, until the thing happened that would make it a tale to be told for as long as people lived in San Ginese.

...

Twenty years passed from the day Tommaso returned from America, and he and Folaino both grew old. Old in those days was different to old now, of course. Nevertheless, they were old.

Tommaso, who was physically very strong, still worked his miserable fields and seemed a man driven by some secret purpose, while Folaino, just as hardy and certainly not poor, rented many of his fields to others and passed the time driving his wife to visit his children and grandchildren. On Sundays the entire family (there were thirty-five of them in total) would appear at Mass in all their opulence. There was a feeling that through their elegant dress and motorcars, and sheer weight of numbers, they were demonstrating their moral superiority to everyone else. Many of us found this irritating and our thoughts would turn sympathetically to Tommaso. This was probably the beginning of his future popularity. Meanwhile, he worked like a dog to scratch a meagre existence from the land and sometimes went just a little hungry.

For twenty years he and Folaino had, generally speaking, managed to avoid each other. On Sundays at Mass, Folaino and his family occupied three pews at the front, while Tommaso sat near the door at the back. Although you could say he was in the ascendancy, Folaino seemed wary of crossing paths with Tommaso after so many years. He always waited for Tommaso to leave before leading his family out.

In the evening Tommaso still came down for his milk, although Irma stopped charging him for it.

...

One day in the middle of summer Tommaso's door creaked open and the old man tottered out, mumbling something to himself and gently shaking his head as if earnestly engaged in conversation with

57

someone. He looked ancient and very tired and was scruffy and grey. He was wearing his clogs. *Clacaclac.* He turned right.

...

After it was all over, the men would sit outside Nedo's bar marvelling at what Tommaso had done. Many did not blame him. They would raise an arm, take their hat off, throw it to the ground and turn away in disgust, making noises such as *pah!* And *mah!* Others would open their right hand to make a dismissive gesture and turn their back on their interlocutors as if sickened by Tommaso's actions. As the years passed, however, there were fewer and fewer who disapproved of him. They remembered Folaino's arrogant display of wealth and his condescension towards those he considered inferior, until finally Tommaso became a hero to all the people of San Ginese. In the end they were prepared to defend him to the death against critical outsiders. He became a kind of patron saint of unlucky migrants, his conduct an example to be followed by anyone who had been badly treated in America.

Some said it must have hurt him terribly to be betrayed by a friend, that he had gone on living as if nothing had happened and suppressed the anger and the resentment and brooded all that time. They imagined Tommaso silently wishing that the person who had hurt him would be hurt. They imagined Tommaso's resentment when he saw that the person who had hurt him was not going to be hurt and the gradually dawning understanding that he would have to be the one to inflict the hurt on Folaino.

Or maybe he had it in for God over the way his life had turned out. He was unmarried, childless, lived with his old maid sisters, and, as Gino said, he was unmoneyed. Folaino was everything he was not. If only he had the money that Folaino had stolen. In the end his patience ran out.

...

Nobody noticed Tommaso as he made his way alone under the canopy of trees alongside the Metato to Folaino's house, where the usually padlocked gate was open, and pounded his fist on the heavy wooden door. When Folaino opened it, Tommaso shot him four times in the chest. *Bang. Bang. Bang. Bang.* Then he turned around and walked home. *Clacaclac.* He was home eating, with renewed appetite, his sad midday meal of cheese and bread with a glass of watered-down wine well before the police arrived and just as the news started spreading.

It was one o'clock on a hot day, and the silent village was at lunch when the troop of police in their smart black uniforms arrived at a jogging pace. There was the clatter and shuffle of swords and running feet. They looked as if they were attending a ceremony on a public holiday, with their white shoulder strings, red-banded trousers, small V-shaped capes and two-cornered hats. Five *carabinieri* knelt in a row behind the low stone wall in front of *le case di sopra* and pointed their guns at the door. When their commanding officer, the *maresciallo*, called out to Tommaso to surrender, there was a long wait, and then the old man calmly walked out. He wasn't muttering to himself now. He was clear-eyed, his skin looked fresher and he seemed to glow.

They handcuffed him and marched him to the lock-up at La Pieve. Those who saw him said that as the procession moved along the top of the San Ginese hill, Tommaso seemed to be at peace with the world, like a man on his deathbed who had made his confession to the priest in plenty of time and was now just waiting for whatever happened next. When they passed the church, the commanding officer told his men to remove the handcuffs, and Tommaso accompanied them freely the rest of the way.

...

Tommaso refused a lawyer throughout the trial and refused to speak in his own defence until the sentence was pronounced. When the judge, in his black cloak, silver and gold cord, shoulder braid and frilly white blouse, asked if he had anything to say, Tommaso rose in the dock and pronounced the words that became legendary in San Ginese. 'Your Honour, I did my duty, nothing more, nothing less.'

And he sat down. The courtroom exploded in applause and cheering.

Tommaso the Killer was given a life sentence but served just five years because he was old and the crime had been committed in a moment of folly. The suggestion that it was premeditated, that he had planned it for twenty years, was incredible, so no-one believed it. Because of his good behaviour and the royal amnesties that were still available at the time, he was released and returned to San Ginese, where he lived a few more good years and died peacefully in his sleep.

Ugo, son of Vitale and Irma, who later emigrated to Australia, lived across the road from Tommaso. He was a boy when all this happened and remembers it very clearly. When his wife, Morena, the daughter of Bucchione, was a little girl, she would visit Tommaso with a crowd of her little friends and knock on his door to hear the famous words.

In fact, in his final years, wherever he went, children and villagers gathered round and someone always called out: 'Tommà, Tommà, what did you to say to the judge, Tommà?'

And Tommà, who by then was ninety years old, would snap to attention and for the thousandth time repeat: 'Your Honour, I did my duty, nothing more, nothing less!'

And everyone would cheer and clap and double over with laughter.

Il Chioccino

The priests of San Ginese were rascals, whoremongers and layabouts. They were men, after all, with the same human desires and weaknesses as everyone else. One parish priest was Don Palagi. Another, who was only a kind of priest, was Il Chioccino, *named for a* chioccia, *which is a brood hen, round and plump. Life in San Ginese was not always wretched.*

In San Ginese, not too long ago, Tista lay dying in his bed. It was the day Ugo went to stand at the foot of the old man's bed, not knowing what to expect. What do you expect to see when they tell you your grandfather is dying and you must go to see him and you are standing at the foot of his bed?

Ugo's sister Lida, the holiest and most religiously observant of the grandchildren, had run up to the church to call the priest.

Tista looked at Ugo and said, 'Ugo, *muoio*.' Just like that.

Ugo looked back at him.

Don Palagi came up the stairs and administered the sacrament of extreme unction.

Tista was at that moment of impending death when the moribund might say, more or less quoting the sixteenth-century poet Pietro Aretino:

> *Son arrivato all'estremo punto*
> *Salvatemi dai topi ora che son unto.*

> I have come to the end time that's appointed
> Save me from the mice now that I'm anointed.

When the priest had finished he left the room rather suddenly, abandoning the family and a few neighbours who were standing around the dying man, and went back downstairs to the kitchen. Ugo's father Vitale told him many years later that he followed the priest and saw him passionately embracing and kissing Rosaria, Drea's wife, who had been distributing food and wine to the visitors.

This was the same priest who refused to bless the houses of families whose relatives had emigrated to Australia. Migrants betrayed their motherland, he said from the pulpit, before announcing that Gianni Di Lilloro, who had been crushed to death in the belt of his wheat thresher the week before, had been punished by God for working on a Sunday.

The priests also carried on as if the feudal entitlement of *jus primae noctis* was still in force throughout the land. It was commonly known that when asked by their distraught and furious husbands on their wedding night who had taken their virginity, local women occasionally replied: 'Go and ask the priest!'

Because we knew about these things, we joked about the men of God. On one occasion Ugo was turning over the soil in the priest's olive grove (this was one of the good works the parishioners did for the priest, a kind of religious obligation everyone shared). He was working alongside Il Tegghio, who was from Marchetti, and who was called that because he looked like a large, round copper pot. At midday they stopped working and the priest's housekeeper, La Chiocca, brought them their food.

Copper Pot asked her, '*Oh, Chiocca, quante ne hai fatto l'altra notte?*' (How many times did you do it last night?)

When the fat old woman blushed (which was a sign of the truth of the accusation), of course the two fell about laughing. She quickly deposited on the ground the two bowls of bean soup she was carrying and waddled off, cursing the men under her breath.

...

Then there was Il Chioccino. Il Chioccino wasn't really a priest. After becoming a man, and working his father's fields for a few years, he became a kind of chaplain and moved to the top of the hill where he shared a house and the housekeeper with the real parish priest. Not that he troubled the housekeeper much, preferring gluttony to lust. He was just a simple peasant at heart and counted his blessings that he had stumbled into this position, which meant he didn't have to do any work while eating well, sleeping as much as he wanted and, at least in his own mind, enjoying the respect of the people in the village.

Many years ago, when Tista was still alive, Irma sent Little Ugo up to the church at Castello to ask the chaplain if he would come to bless the onions in the field, which were being eaten by worms. Ugo knocked on the door of the presbytery and the chaplain opened it. He listened to Ugo, all the while wiping breadcrumbs from his chin and emitting a gassy concoction of onions and wine, either from a bodily orifice or from the pores of his skin, or maybe from both. Il Chioccino agreed to perform the sacred ritual the next day.

With his little terrier in tow, he arrived just before one o'clock, as Irma was setting the table. Vitale, who was in the vineyard, dropped his shovel and joined them in the patch of land below the house, removing his hat as he took his place beside Ugo and Irma, who had come running from the kitchen, draping a scarf over her head. They stood there on the edge of the onion row with their heads bowed and hands piously joined as Il Chioccino read out the church-sanctioned official Blessing of the Onions. As the dog raised its leg on a clod of earth, Ugo wondered whether, as the blessing took effect, the worms would feel any pain and if they would actually die, or whether they would just retreat and wriggle over to eat Julio the Orphan's carrots five metres away.

Having completed his work for the day, Il Chioccino folded his arms inside the long sleeves of his cassock and stood there nodding, looking at the other three, smiling, a little round man who resembled the small wine barrels people had in their cellars. The church bell tolled one o'clock. Irma looked at Vitale and Vitale looked back at her, and Irma looked at the assistant priest, who looked at her. She invited him to stay for the midday meal. Il Chioccino's face exploded with happiness. His meal for the day was assured! What a heavenly profession God had chosen for him!

And so he stayed and ate and drank and was still there late in the afternoon, showing no sign of leaving, when the sun started to set behind the hill on the side of the house. Vitale had excused himself to return to the vineyard, and it was left to Irma and Tista to entertain the chaplain with conversation and one glass of wine after another, accompanied by pecorino cheese and bread. It was so late that it was getting cold, so Tista lit a fire with twigs and kindling kept in a large, heavy wicker basket beside the fireplace.

In order to warm himself in front of what was soon a crackling, spitting inferno, Il Chioccino wobbled to his feet and, taking a few steps towards the basket, went to sit down on its edge. The basket was too low, not heavy or stable enough, and he was too fat, too round and unsteady after three flasks of Vitale's wine, so as he lowered his body and allowed himself to drop the last few centimetres, instead of coming to rest on the edge he fell into the middle of the container, where his backside found a perfectly snug fit. And there he stuck, firmly planted, doubled up, his face buried in his crotch, his legs wriggling, arms waving.

Tista took him by an arm and tried to haul him out but only ended up dragging him and the basket in a circle around the kitchen table. The little black-and-white-spotted dog Il Chioccino had brought with him became very excited and began yapping at his master while keeping a safe distance until, who knows what came over him, he charged in and bit his master's fat thigh and retreated under the table, where he continued barking.

By rolling him onto his side, one of them pulling him by the head while the other held the basket, Irma and Tista finally freed him. Of course, after that they had to give him another glass of wine to calm his nerves, and some prosciutto and bread to settle his stomach, which had become agitated in all the excitement. Irma was worried he was going to stay for dinner, but he had already eaten and drunk so much that in the end he seemed glad to leave. She asked Ugo to accompany him up the hill to his home near the church and so the little boy took Il Chioccino home, walking a little in front of him and trying hard to ignore the sounds that came whenever the assistant priest made a special effort on the steeper parts. Ugo watched him collapse onto his little bed and go straight to sleep as he wished the boy goodnight, emitting one final, prolonged trumpet blast.

In the end the onions were saved, but Ugo always wondered if it was really Almighty God's intervention in the sad little field below the house or just the weather and other circumstances.

The only good thing you could say about a priest was that he visited all the dying, as if to say it didn't matter whether you were rich or poor, famous or unknown. In the end God treated you all in the same way.

Nevertheless, the people of San Ginese have never had much respect for their priests.

Bucchione and the Angel
of Sadness

On the day he turned ten, Bucchia, as he was called then, finished building himself a small wooden cart that he rode down the hill from Clementina's place and along the main street, the only street, of Villora. He rumbled past the house on the right where Nedo, who was Nedo's father, would one day open the village bar next to Gino's place and charge twenty lire to watch television in a special room at the back. The boy sped past the plot of land on the left that would later become Neva's garden (built halfway down into the ditch where Derì's motorcycle landed after the Dinner of the Pig), bounced through the dip in the road at the bend and headed straight into Beàno. Planting the heels of his shoes firmly in the dirt, he ground to a chaotic jumble of a stop in a cloud of dust and a scatter of gravel outside Lilì's house. Then he dragged his cart back up to the top and started again. He did this over and over all day, and no-one took any notice because he was just a little boy playing with his little wooden cart.

The late springtime sun setting behind the Montanari hill left Villora in shadow as Bucchia's father, Paolino, his arm outstretched over the handle of the scythe resting on his shoulder, walked home from the Preselle field. He proceeded at that infinitely patient pace that peasants invented and still observe all over the world and that city people wish they could imitate. It's the kind of pace that says, *I am alive and have worked hard today and the earth has been good to me. I am enjoying the walk that will see me home where I can rest my bones.*

Rounding the bend behind the house, Paolino heard the crunch of gravel and the boy shrieking at the top of his voice. He waited for him in front of Lilì's house, and the next time Bucchia arrived from his run he grabbed him by the shoulder, spun him around and told him to stop because he was tiring himself out and getting hot and sweaty and everybody knew this was not good for children. Bucchia hung his head, dropped his chin onto his chest and stuck out his bottom lip. Paolino went down to the stable to milk and feed the cows.

As soon as his father was out of sight, the little boy wiped the disappointment from his face so that it looked as if the sun had just come up in his eyes. He decided he would do the run a few more times, to see if he could go faster. Paolino heard the boy still at it. He finished his work and waited for him.

While little Bucchia pleaded with him, using the formal form of address with parents, which was common then, '*Non me lo rompete! Non me lo rompete!*', Paolino chopped the cart up with an axe. No-one would have believed him capable of doing something like that.

...

Because of the presence of the nearby swamp and the damp, fetid air, Bucchia, like every other child in the village, had weak lungs and often caught bronchitis, so every year in summer Paolino and Teresa took him to the seaside at Viareggio to breathe the fresh salt air. When he was old, he remembered those visits and spoke of seeing fishermen's huts made of cane and straw on the viale Margherita. This is the now glamorous Liberty-era beachfront avenue, where smartly dressed men and women stroll arm in arm as music from café orchestras drifts out through the wide open French doors onto the crowded footpaths.

The Mediterranean breeze had the desired medicinal effect, and Bucchia grew tall and robust and was renamed Bucchione by the villagers.

...

God had made Bucchione so strong that whenever he was confronted by a difficulty he either smashed it, lifted it up, carried it away or dug a hole and buried it. For example, if the obstacle was his sadness, first he transferred the sadness into a pile of manure, or a field of hay or corn. Then he worked his way through it, shovelling the manure, loading the hay onto a cart with a pitchfork, or harvesting the corn, filling fifty sacks and carrying them home five at a time.

He did the same thing if he was concerned about some matter. When he was troubled at the thought of leaving his family alone and defenceless while he went to the war, he decided to plant a new vineyard behind the house. By the time the vines had sprouted small green shoots (and by the time he had fooled the authorities into classifying him as unfit for military service) the fear was gone and his life was normal again.

In those days, as always, there were a number of sightings of the Angel of Sadness in San Ginese, and the villagers tried all kinds of strategies to avoid it. Some men ran away to America, scores of them scurrying aboard ships in Genoa, hoping to leave the Angel behind, but when they came back they found it waiting for them at their front doors. A very few, like Paolino, ran away a second time, but even that didn't help. Paolino had been to America twice, and both times had come back poorer than when he left, a feat unequalled in the district and a profound lesson for Bucchione, who never travelled further than Corsica in search of work.

The villagers who remained behind sought ways of keeping the Angel at bay. They spent longer hours in the fields and stables and at the bar, drank more *ponce* (the name given to a small glass of strong coffee, with a splash of rum, a dash of sugar and a slice of lemon peel), played more card games or smoked more cigars, looking for consolation in the perfume and pull of the tobacco.

Whenever he heard the satin whisper of angel wings behind him and felt the air move where there should have been no movement, Bucchione worked harder, developing a capacity for sustained labour that became legendary.

Given his father Paolino's spectacular failures in America, Bucchione was never inspired to cross the Atlantic in search of his fortune, but from the age of sixteen, every autumn for twenty years the big man would catch the ferry across to Corsica to work, returning in the spring.

The story goes that when he was in Corsica, armed with just a shovel and an axe, he excavated a kilometre-long trench, drained a swamp, dug up an entire plain and chopped down a forest. One day, on a farm near Bastia, he was digging in a field when the owner of the farm asked him to stop because there was other work to do. Bucchione, whom God, we know already, had made strong, was born to use a shovel, and the soil was so soft and easy to work that he forgot the instruction and kept digging, turning the clods over and moving down the field. The owner reminded him again, telling him to finish the furrow and then get on with the other job, but

Bucchione wanted to see how long it would take him to finish the whole field. Finally the boss pulled out a large pistol and pointed it at him and said, 'Stop now, *monsieur*, or I will spread you all over that chestnut tree.'

In Corsica he also worked in a quarry and on road construction gangs. Large rocks from the quarry were placed at regular intervals by the side of the road and workers like Bucchione made their way along, slowly smashing them into smaller and smaller pieces, ultimately pulverising them, chipping away with hammers of various sizes, including the small rock hammer he later gave to Ugo when Ugo worked on the construction of the tunnel through the mountain between Lucca and Pisa before he left for Australia. This is the mountain that, according to Dante, in Canto XXXIII of the Inferno, prevents the Pisans from seeing Lucca.

Bucchione was by far the hardest worker in the district and spread more stone chips and pulverised more rock over a road surface than anyone else. He often worked bare-chested, even when it snowed. One year it was so cold that the moisture on his top lip started to freeze and only the warm air he breathed out through his nostrils prevented the formation of light crumbs of ice. He had to keep breathing out to stop his lips solidifying. Bucchione sat half-naked on a rock, on a mountainside in Corsica, chipping away, building the road, stubborn and strong, while the snowflakes glided down from the sky and settled on him.

In San Ginese, he became a mythical character as the years passed. It was said that once, in a single day, he carried two motherless calves to their wet-nurse in a neighbouring village and then ran home and loaded twenty 54-litre demijohns of wine onto a merchant's carts as if they were feather-filled pillows. For those who do not know, a demijohn is a large, round-bodied, wicker-covered blown-glass container originating in Damghan in Persia, called a *damigiana* in San Ginese and throughout Italy. Then he rescued the team of working cows that his now elderly father Paolino had allowed to slide off the edge of a field into an irrigation ditch, where the poor beasts were stuck in mud up to their shoulders, and when they refused to go any further he hitched himself up to the hay cart and pulled it home himself with the cows meekly trailing behind, looking quite ashamed. At such times he became lost in a rapture that did not leave him until the work was done.

Bucchione was also renowned for the strength of his convictions, his righteous anger and his hot temper. With one punch he flattened the nose of a trespasser from Centoni whose cow, a large, white, small-horned Tuscan Chianina, was eating his lush green pasture in the Preselle field. He scolded the beast, which was immediately penitent, and made it lead the miserable human offender home. Bucchione later sent Gino to make peace with the man and his family and the cow. The rage in his eyes made men afraid, but after it passed he was like a lamb. He was sympathetic to murderers and other criminals when he believed they were applying their own rough justice in a corrupt society where the privileged and the higher class ruled.

As a young man he worked as a day labourer on the Maggiorello hill, which in those days was covered with vineyards and olive groves. He later bought a vineyard there and produced some of the best wine in the district. The hillside was positioned so that the morning sun rose behind it from Porcari and received the rays of the afternoon sun, which set on the San Leonardo side. His Australian grandson helped him tie vines. For lunch there was bread and cheese, perhaps a pear each, a bottle of water and a flask of wine.

By the time they were old, both he and his sister Gemma were toothless. His gums became very bony and hard, and he could chew almost anything. He was still strong and had great stamina when loading a hay cart or moving demijohns of wine about in the cellar. On the way home from cutting hay, with Bucchione in charge of the cow, Gemma, with her pointed nose and sunken mouth, would perch on top of the hay cart wearing her perennial headscarf, looking like a rapacious bird.

His Tuscan cigar was planted permanently in the corner of his mouth. Occasionally he would light it. About him wafted the acrid smell of stale cow manure, made sweet with the perfume of straw.

At the small kitchen table that seated the entire family of eight (when the Australians were visiting), Bucchione kept a wine flask and a leg of prosciutto in a basket on the floor beside him, filling glasses and slicing and presenting the salted, preserved pork to others on the end of a pointy knife, all on request. His wine was light red or cloudy white and sweet, friendly to drink, with tiny, light, natural bubbles.

After the midday meal, which always started at one o'clock and was over by two, he would shuffle off to the village bar wearing a white singlet, a collarless flannel shirt with all its buttons undone, a worn blue jacket draped over his shoulders, blue canvas trousers held up by a piece of string for a belt and an old brown trilby with a greasy sweat stain running around it, his slippers scraping on the gravel path. He never became a bent old man but maintained his upright bearing and its emotional counterpart, a positive disposition, until the very end.

His Australian grandson helped him shovel corn into sacks, filling them with dusty grains that had been spread over a broken concrete yard to air and dry in the sun. If you are visiting and listen carefully, you can still hear the shovel scraping on the ground.

The Flour-Eater and the Girl Without a Reflection

Bucchione married Iose Dal Porto, Derì's sister, who was from Centoni and had unusual eating habits. By the time she had completed her eighteenth year she had been courted by two young men but had quickly grown tired of both of them. Bucchione was impressed by her reputation for hard work in the fields, a reputation she had developed from an early age. She was smitten with his size and looks, although, as it turned out, this applied only as long as she wasn't required to make physical contact with him.

Delicate and ladylike in her youth, despite her large, square, masculine fingers, Iose was accustomed to a comfortable life with indulgent parents. She had her own pretty carriage, which she hitched to a nervous little pony to tour the villages on Sundays after Mass while showing off a new dress. Skittish like her horse, which bolted once and at breakneck speed carried her two kilometres along the ridge of the San Ginese hill, she ran away and went back home three days into her marriage to the large and boisterous Bucchione, who frightened her with his size and strength. Within a week she was back, reluctantly, but never really felt at home in Villora, and always pined for Centoni and the gentleness of her father's house, for white satin lace and frilly dresses, for her doting mother, for her two sisters and her sweet, melancholy brother.

Nevertheless, she helped train the young heifers as working cows, and grew beans, onions, carrots and cardoons, which she sold at the market in Lucca. The vegetables were grown in the family's fields at *la Botra*, also known as *il Bozzo*, a pond on a spring near Pierini that had eels in it.

Early in the morning, when it was still dark, she and her son, little Paolo, would load the bicycle with baskets and bags full of the current season's crop and head off to the Piazza dell'Anfiteatro. On arriving she would claim a good position near one of the archways leading into the big open space that had once been a Roman amphitheatre. Over hundreds of years, houses had been built up against the amphitheatre's outer walls, and as it had fallen into decay and eventually been demolished, the houses around its perimeter remained, leaving empty the oval shape it had once occupied, and forming a communal area perfectly suited for a market. Iose would spread out a large canvas sheet and arrange the produce in small, neat piles, with the most attractive samples on top. She was an expert haggler, a skill she inherited from her father, the farm broker.

Later, as the agricultural economy began to die, she took in knitting like her sister Alfonsina, and they became outworkers for one of those new factories they were building, as did many other women in the village. She too kept the sadness at bay by working hard. No other woman made as many pieces of knitwear – jumper sleeves, fronts and backs – in a day as she did.

The Flour-Eater had two major defects.

The first flaw was that she never ate a plate of spaghetti or polenta, or a vegetable or a piece of meat in her life, and never touched sweets. She lived on a diet of cheese and a mixture made of milk and wheat flour, to which she would add a few olives, which also found their way into her coffee. While the rest of the family was at the table feasting on Gemma's renowned rabbit stew, she would be at the stove, a few feet away, stirring the milk and adding bread and flour to thicken it. Because she did not enjoy food, she was unable to cook. The thought of preparing a meal that she could not bear to eat brought her to despair, and if you put her in the kitchen she would panic.

The second imperfection was brought by the Angel of Sadness. It had visited her in Centoni one night soon after she was born. It followed her around for the rest of her life, and she struggled to prevent it from overwhelming her. By throwing herself into her work she barely managed to keep it at bay. Although she did not inherit any of her father's estate, Giuseppe dei Centoni did bequeath to her his powerful variations of humour. At times of powerful emotion – for example, after giving birth to her first child, Morena, who later emigrated to Australia – she became a sad rag, lost all desire to live and remained in bed for weeks. She gradually resumed her knitting work to help support the family, but remained forever sadder than she was previously. The birth of her second child, Paolo, brought on a recurrence of the earlier condition. Her life was a prolonged sadness for her and for all those around her.

...

Just as Giuseppe Giovannoni was known as Bucchione, so was his sister Gemma Giovannoni known as Galgani.

The real Saint Gemma Galgani was from Lucca, which was just down the road from San Ginese, and because Gemma Giovannoni was a hard-working, patient and selfless creature, everyone associated her with the saint and called her Galgani. All her life she never travelled further than the few kilometres to Lucca, and was the happiest person anyone who knew her had ever met. She was not an overly devout woman, simply observing the major religious services. Gemma understood there was an Australia because she knew there was an America that half the village had been to. She wondered if Australians had chickens and electricity.

Gemma appeared to be perfectly content with her life, and if you asked her the secret to her happiness, she would say it was that she did not have a reflection. At this, most people would smile inside their hearts and look at her with sympathy and condescension.

When she first looked in the mirror as a young girl her reflection appeared to her very faint, although to her mother and anyone else standing beside her the reflection was perfectly normal. As she grew older, her reflection became even fainter until, on her sixteenth birthday, it disappeared. She had not seen herself since then, although everyone else could see her, quite clearly. As time passed, however, the rest of the village also started to believe she had no reflection, and after a time hardly anyone would test the belief by standing beside her in front of the mirror. The word spread and soon those who did see a reflection were suspected of being sinners and of having blackened souls. And so her sainthood grew.

Gemma washed the family's clothes and linen at the communal laundry in the stream that flowed past Vitale's spring. She cooked meals, gathered edible weeds from the fields and paths, raised and slaughtered chickens and rabbits, sowed and planted and picked corn and other vegetables, loaded hay carts, milked and fed the cows. She ran the household, taking charge of all the domestic chores, teaching Morena to cook, raising her and Paolo as if they were her own children.

She had had one half-hearted suitor in her youth, but decided men were too much trouble and quickly lost what little interest she had.

When it turned out that Iose, the woman her brother had married, was an ineffective wife and mother, Gemma assumed the relevant responsibilities. She became the wise spinster sister, who cared for the elderly parents and the young children and was generally in command of the domestic aspects of the household. She discussed important family matters with Bucchione, who always consulted her.

Gemma had a favourite saying that she repeated at every opportunity to anyone who complained about the state of their life: *Bisogna mangiare tre sacca di polvere prima di morire* (by the time you die you will have eaten three sacks of dust). It was clear this meant that life is long and hard, and if you think you have problems now, be prepared to put up with a lot more.

Gemma died of pneumonia in the new hospital in Lucca, the first of the family not to die at home, in her own bed. The vision of those who saw her last is of a thin, haggard woman with tubes protruding from her nose and mouth far away on the other side of a window in a sterile isolation ward. She had suffered all her life from *ipertiroidismo*, which kept her extremely thin, even skeletal. In fact, this was probably why men did not look at her. This, and the fact that she had a strong personality.

Buona Fortuna!

Ugo's father and grandfather and half the village had been to America. They hated San Ginese for the poverty and the mud and the cow shit and the pig shit. The Sanginesini took to going to America with such fervour that it was as though they had been waiting for her to rise up on the other side of the ocean ever since God had made His promise to the chosen.

It was as if the Lord had said, 'I have seen the misery of my people in San Ginese. I have heard them crying out and I am concerned about their suffering. So I have come to rescue them and show them the road to a good and spacious land, a land flowing with milk and honey. So now, go. Go to America. Bring yourselves out of misery.'

...

When he's a little boy he listens to them talking about America, those who have been and come back, and he starts to dream. He hears the words from the Bible about the milk and the honey and the streets paved with gold.

The shipping agents visit the villages and give away postcards depicting giant chickens, monstrous carrots, colossal cattle and silver coins growing on trees, and he sees these images in the tavern as the men pass them around. This is what he will have in America. Everything there is abundant.

He's a dreamer and reads books by the light emanating from his *lumino*, a beautiful word for a round tin lid filled with olive oil, in which rests a strip of linen for a wick, burning its small flickering flame on a saucer on the chair beside his bed in his nook under the stairs.

· · ·

Eight men sit around a table in the tavern, sucking their cigars and drinking their sweet coffee and rum with a sliver of lemon peel. While four of them watch, another four play, slamming their cards down with a shout, shooting gobs of phlegm into a strategically placed spittoon and telling stories about their time in America.

One of the old men curses the ship that brought him back to the pile of mud and shit that is the village in Tuscany called San Ginese. *Oh, that it had sunk, that curséd vessel that brought me back to this pile of mud and shit!*

The old man speaks of the horrible storms they brave as they sail from Genoa, out of the Mediterranean Sea, through the Pillars of Hercules at Gibraltar, and across what is really just a short distance to New York. The waves are so high and the troughs so deep and the ship leans so hard that you can wash your hands in the ocean as it rises before you like a sudden mountain.

There is work in America, as much as you want, thick wads of green banknotes at the end of the working week, freedom to move on, if you don't like the boss, and always another job to go to.

· · ·

And they would go to America and become lost over there, and when they returned to San Ginese they would still be lost, as if they could not find the place they had left but kept looking for it, anywhere, somewhere, but it was always elsewhere – on top of a hill, along the walking paths between the villages, in a field, inside a stable or a pig-sty, inside a woman, a wife, a neighbour's wife. You could see the men wandering about in the courtyards and between the houses, aimlessly at first, and then slowly they would give the appearance of settling into their lives again, but remained as sad as trees that have had half their roots hacked off. Such trees can barely feed and water themselves and are in danger of toppling over in the gentlest breeze.

At night, after their card game, they shuffled stiffly out into the mud and went home. As they slumbered restlessly in their beds, dreaming of the America they had lost, their laments could be heard above the snoring of the cows and rabbits, the heavy breathing of the chickens and the snorting of the pigs (who never slept, for fear of the butcher's skewer). The wives of the returned men hardly slept at all.

With their hearts set on regret, the men tossed and turned and woke their wives, who by morning were tired and sad and pitied by the women whose husbands had never left and slept the deep sleep of the innocent.

The road to America is hard.

Yes, they went to America and yes, they made money, if they were lucky, but their hearts broke. They caught a disease, a deep sadness that afflicted soldiers fighting away from home, soldiers who were otherwise fit, a *homesickness* that killed them, whether they stayed or returned home.

...

Ugo married and his first son was born and he, the wife and the child all lived in his father's house with his father, mother, two brothers, one sister-in-law and one nephew. His young wife wasn't happy, and threw a broomstick at her mother-in-law and walked out with the baby to her own parents' house, one hundred metres away.

Ugo's older brother had taken the spare cow and the fields that their father had bought with American money. There were not enough cows and fields left to support Ugo's family.

So there he was, restless and empty and bored, living days without routine, his life frittered away, almost gone. The *lumino* burned and spluttered and flickered gently in a tin lid filled with olive oil.

Then, because the Americans had closed their doors, he wrote to the Canadians and the Australians. The Australians wrote back immediately. There was scarcity in Australia, there was a famine; the country hungered for people and demanded to be fed.

So he packed a few things into one famous suitcase.

...

On the day Ugo left San Ginese it snowed, and the road up near Clementina's house had iced over. It hardly ever snowed in San Ginese, so this was a day he never forgot. During the night the snow had covered the whole world, including the roof of the pink house at Gan-Gan, on the flank of the hill on the right, which had been bombed during the war. The snow had formed small heaps on the steps in front of Clementina's, where Bucchione started his run down into Beàno in the little wooden cart that his father Paolino then chopped up with an axe.

He paid Giuseppe Dal Porto to drive him to the train in Lucca, and Bucchione and Sucker went with him.

The road out of San Ginese up to the crossroads winds twice, sharply, and is very steep. Albo the milkman had been doing the milk-collection round with his donkey, which had five large churns strapped to its sides and was now climbing towards the top of the Speranza hill.

Giuseppe Dal Porto blew the horn as the car approached. The donkey was struggling to maintain its footing on the frozen bitumen and kept falling onto its backside, performing a kind of frenetic four-hoofed dance.

'Ugo, *buona fortuna*,' Albo called out, waving, as the car crawled past. '*Buona fortuna!*'

THE ENCHANTED GLADE
AND THE BABBLING BROOK

The Fireflies of Autumn

When the war came to San Ginese, the people had been expecting it for many years, although it still took everyone by surprise.

It started like this.

In the days when the Union of Soviet Socialist Republics, the Unione delle Repubbliche Socialiste Sovietiche, or URSS, was the hope of the oppressed peoples of the world, and Benito Mussolini's fascist government signed the Lateran treaties with the Catholic Church (this was in 1929), Bucchione had not yet married Iose the Flour-Eater, and he lived in *casa vecchia* with Paolino and Teresa (his mother and father), and his sisters, Gemma and Orsolina. Alongside the staircase leading from the hallway to the bedrooms on the first floor, there was a lighter patch of plaster that didn't match the rest of the wall.

In San Ginese a squad of fascists wearing black shirts was doing the rounds of the villages looking for evidence of hostility to the regime. Bucchione, who was an unashamed communist, hated the fascists and hated the church, and the fact that they had now signed an agreement recognising and supporting each other in Rome doubled the hatred he felt.

Being no patriot, he saw the coming war as a class struggle. Later he was unimpressed with jokes about the cowardice of Italian soldiers, given that for him so-called cowardice was a means of self-preservation for the good of your family. Italy had been ravaged by many invaders over the centuries, and to him Mussolini was just another invader.

He had drawn a hammer and sickle on the wall alongside the staircase at the back of the front room, an act of defiance and a manifestation of his political allegiance, but now the *camicie nere*, the black shirts, were going around banging on doors and they were bound to see it and there would be trouble.

Four of them came one night, calling at every house in Villora. When you opened the door they strode in as if they owned the place, sounding friendly in a bold and jovial kind of way, until they detected something they didn't like, either in the tone of your voice or the attitude of your body. Once they had decided you were hostile to the government, they punished you by pouring castor oil through a funnel down your throat, and, if you were unlucky, gave you a few blows around the ribs with a stick. Muffled cries, the scraping of chairs dragged along stone floors and thumping, banging, knocking noises travelled through the walls of all the houses in the village and down into the foundations made of human bones, because, as you know, Villora was built on top of the cemetery of a medieval monastery.

When she heard from Nedo at the bar that they were coming, Gemma ran to get the lime they used to dust the vines and mixed it with water to make a paste, which she spread with her hands over the communist symbol on the wall, to cover it up before the bastards knocked on the door. That part of the wall would forever be discoloured, but that night in the dark little house the fascists would not notice. While she was seeing to this, Gemma grumbled about men and how they needlessly complicated everybody's lives with politics and war and other fancy ideas. Sometimes she thought the women and children of San Ginese would be better off without them.

Bucchione opened the door and invited them in. One of them was Michelino, the son of the butcher and an old family friend, and Bucchione greeted him with a hug and a slap on the back. Creusa's father was there too, who had been a foundling, and Venanzio, Drea's father. Bucchione didn't know the other man.

He offered them all a glass of wine, and pulled a fresh ham off the hook and started slicing while Gemma fetched bread. He said nice things about *il Duce*, including how good it was that the swamp had been drained and the malaria eliminated, and pretty soon the visitors' bellies were full and they were all in a jovial mood, feeling welcome after receiving cool receptions in every other house.

As Gemma hurried back into the front room carrying the bread basket, head bowed inside her headscarf, she glanced sideways at her brother, who, unseen by the uninvited guests, winked.

This was the story that, as an old man, Bucchione told his young Australian grandson. Bucchione was no fool. He knew it wasn't important to win small victories when there was a greater battle to be fought and won, the battle for your life and for the wellbeing of your family. The thugs would go away and leave you alone if you filled their bellies and made the right noises. The time would come when the people would take care of the men in black shirts. But first there would have to be a war.

...

When the war came to San Ginese, it was autumn and the days were shorter, and in the mornings the mist rose out of the dry swamp and floated away into the sky. In the evenings it rolled down from the hills and crawled into the empty spaces between the trees, lay gently on the fields, rolled over onto its back, turning to one side and then the other, holding the entire plain in its ghostly embrace until the world to the east, this side of Porcari, was a dirty grey translucent smudge and the only sign of hope was the sickly pale-yellow halo of the electric light at the Baracca tavern, where the villagers from nearby Picchio, who were renowned layabouts, ate fried eels, played *briscola*, drank wine all night and slept all day while their crops rotted in abandoned fields and their animals starved in the stables.

In Villora the smoke from the poplar logs burning in the fireplaces refused to rise above the rooftops. It drifted around the houses, settling somewhere between your nose and your eyes so that it blinded you; it smarted inside your nostrils and made you weep and sneeze. The tall men of the village looked down along the blanket of smoke hovering below their chins and saw furry rodents gliding past in a ghostly silver sea, illuminated by the single streetlight on the corner in front of Gino's house. Sometimes a hat or a woman's thick locks sailed into view; other times it was a procession of lustrous pates and wisps of hair slicked wetly onto balding craniums.

With the cooling of the season the women prepared thick vegetable soups, throwing in the few remaining pieces of salted pork from last year's pig that were stored in large terracotta jars. In December the new pig would be killed, but for now they made do with the remnants of the old one. The tang of black cabbage, onions, beans and pork filled Beàno, the Winds, Canaponi, the Houses Above, the Mattei Courtyard and Il Sasso.

...

When the war came to San Ginese, all one hundred and twenty inhabitants of Villora were shocked, including Bucchione. For weeks he had swaggered about, proclaiming that the armies would not come close to the village, which, according to him, was just a pile of manure near the bottom of the San Ginese hill.

'Everyone knows that!' he roared. 'Although we're fortunate to be the first village to receive the morning sun, all this means is that by evening we stink more than the others. In summer the sun brings our cesspits to boiling point and bakes our compost heaps of cow manure and straw. Even now, in autumn, we can still smell every stone in the village impregnated with the shit of a thousand summers. The Germans and the Americans know this and will go out of their way to avoid us. The reek of excrement will be Villora's salvation!'

The shit of a thousand summers! The reek of excrement! People looked at one another wide-eyed, shook their heads and marvelled at his poetic gift.

Bucchione made this announcement one afternoon, standing on the low wall in front of Lilì's place, where a small group had gathered to enjoy the breeze blowing up from Porcari. As he spoke he raised his right arm, like Vladimir Lenin in the famous statue.

'Which army would bother coming through here?' he continued. 'They will go right past us, down the main road on the San Leonardo side.'

Toothless Beo – whose nickname meant 'worm', whose real name was Vincenzo Giovannoni, and who had a malfunctioning thyroid gland that made him look like a skinny white maggot – took advantage of the spell that Bucchione was casting over his small audience to plant his hand between Bruna's cold buttocks and give the left one a good squeeze. Bruna, pretending to adjust the scarf on her head, let Beo feel the back of her hand across his face, and Bucchione, noticing a small commotion at the back of the group, hesitated a moment but ploughed on.

'We only need to look out for stray mortars and artillery shells. The Wehrmacht, that great German war machine, will not come anywhere near us, and as for the American Fifth, well, why would they bother with this pile of shit?'

He flung open his arms as if to embrace the mountain of manure that was the courtyard and its houses, inviting the villagers to see for themselves what a pile of shit everything was. Lilì felt reassured. Bucchione made sense. The best way out of trouble was not to get into it in the first place, and if the armies avoided San Ginese, well, the villagers had nothing to fear. She nodded and emitted a supportive sound, which the others heard and took up, nodding and grunting at one another until in the end even Bucchione thought they were overdoing it, although he didn't know how to make them stop.

...

Within a week of Bucchione's speech, two stray bombs hit the village. The armies had installed themselves in the surrounding hills and started shooting at one another.

One night Nello the idiot, who had a vivid imagination, ran around knocking on doors announcing that the fireflies were back. 'Come, come, come and look! Fireflies, fireflies – the fireflies have returned! Fireflies, fireflies!'

Fireflies belonged to the summer, when they were born, lived a short life and died. It was rare to find fireflies flitting about in autumn. Yet there they were, the pretty little bugs, on the Montanari hill where the Americans had set up their battery. Tiny lights dancing in the distance accompanied by the *pop pop pop* of exploding shells and the occasional burst of machine-gun fire.

One shell blew away two-thirds of the pretty pink villa at Gan-Gan, where thirty years later the Milanese would bring their weekend whores, and the Dead Boy and his Australian friend would drink whisky and brandy dregs and watch the sun rise over Porcari. The second bomb flattened the house built by Gimi, who would become the father of the Dead Boy. Sirio, Norato's brother, who was just eighteen years old, was sauntering past and lost both his legs and his private parts and died shortly after, which everyone said was a blessing.

The explosion that killed Sirio sent half the village running to the bomb shelter. The rest hid in wine cellars and haystacks, where the only danger was a direct hit, and no-one in Villora was ever that unlucky (except Sirio, of course).

With Villora in the hollow between them, the German artillery at Castello fired at the American outpost on top of the Montanari hill. The Americans fired right back. The shells screamed overhead from one side to the other, backwards and forwards. It was as if the missile that was sent across was being promptly returned by the enemy. There was even a certain monotony about it, so that the occasional misdirected stray, with its unique whistling sound, was a welcome relief.

Whenever a bomb fell short, it would frighten everyone and they would scramble into the cave under Lilì's house. Bucchione, still smarting from the embarrassment of his inaccurate prediction about the progress of the war, dragged large branches and rolled massive rocks across the entrance until they all felt safe in the dark in the hole under the hill. It was the least he could do.

Apart from working in the fields and stables, there wasn't much for the people in the village to do except tell one another stories, and of course some storytellers were better than others. Bulletta was one of the best.

(It is well known in San Ginese that Bulletta was given that name when, as a boy, he swallowed a nail. *Bulletta* is the local word for nail, replacing the standard Italian word, which is *chiodo*. After he swallowed the nail his mother sat him on a chamber-pot and, from time to time, to encourage him to excrete it, cried out: '*Caca la bulletta! Caca la bulletta!*' The entire village heard her cries and the little boy from that moment on was known as Bulletta.)

So, on the day Sirio was blown apart, once the large crowd had settled into the cave, Treccia, who was squatting as usual on his haunches, chewing a cigar and spitting in the dirt between his feet, called out, 'Ehi, Bullé, tell us the story of the nails!'

And Bulletta did.

'Mengale, also known as Pasquin Della Pompa, was a funny little man from Centoni. He had two small, fat, pretty daughters and a son called Elio. You remember Mengale, don't you? He was so short he was unable to ride a bicycle because his feet couldn't reach the pedals. Anyway, he was tired of having to buy nails from the blacksmith. He thought it was ridiculous to pay someone for such a small thing as a nail when with a little diligence you could grow your own.

'And so he decided to grow his own.

'He dug a patch in a part of his vegetable garden half obscured by a large poplar, so that no-one would see it. He carefully turned his best manure into the soil, and planted the nails with the sharp end facing the sky. *That's how you plant nails*, he thought, *the pointy end towards Heaven, up where they want to grow, pointing to God, who might look down and smile on them.* Then he watered them and waited. He was certain each nail seed would produce a bush laden with bunches of fully formed nails, which he might even sell to the blacksmith in large quantities. He would even become the blacksmith's supplier and perhaps export them to America, where there was a lot of construction of buildings and railroads, or so he had heard.

'Every day he checked the crop for worms, which, as you know, are a big problem in San Ginese, but the nails were unaffected. Meanwhile, his onion crop, just two metres away, was being destroyed by tiny nematodes that not even the parish priest's blessing of the onions had been able to get rid of.

'He checked his crop every day, pretending he was visiting his devastated onion field and his carrots, when actually he was glancing out of the corner of his eye at the rows and rows of nails, which seemed to be making slow progress, if they were making any at all. He poured more liquid manure on the crop, and spread more straw and cow shit between the seedlings.

'One day a few weeks after the planting, he walked through the bed of nails to see whether they were ready to harvest and, accidentally standing on a few of them, was shocked to find how hard and sharp they were under the soles of his feet. That's when the yelps started. The entire village, from Clementina's down to Bucchione's, heard him cursing and screaming from the pain. It seemed he would go on forever. When the lightning bolts in his feet stopped, he decided he would keep to himself the discovery that the nails now were well and truly ready to harvest, although not in the form of bunches on bushes as he had expected.

'He quickly brought in his crop, filling an entire basket, which he hid in a corner of his stable. Mengale grew several more crops and soon found that nails would grow at any time of the year, needed very little water or fertiliser, and were unaffected by moulds, worms or insects. They also stored very well, and were not troubled by plagues of mice, which seemed to ignore them.

'However, he was puzzled. No matter how abundantly he watered the crop, no matter how carefully he spread his best manure, the rich golden-brown liquid *perugino* and the rotten compost from the heap outside his stable, the harvest was always modest. After growing three crops in succession and carefully studying the size of each harvest, he decided that nails, while full of promise as a cash crop, were not profitable.

'Unlike most other harvests, whose yield either exceeded or did not meet expectations, the harvest of nails was always the same.

'You could never reap more than you planted!'

Out of the dark, from the depths of the makeshift bomb shelter, came cries of 'Poor Mengale!' and 'What an idiot!'

'It's true! It's true!' said someone else.

'I can vouch for it. It's all true. It really happened!' replied another.

'I saw him and I heard him suffer the tortures of hell.'

'And he thought none of us knew!'

'Poor short little Mengale!'

As everyone fell about laughing hysterically at the story of Mengale, plump-buttocked Bruna lit a candle and kept an eye on Beo, with his wandering hands. In the silence that followed the general hilarity, the flickering light caught and held the attention of the Sanginesini. They all looked around at one another's distorted facial features and wondered whether their friends had become monsters. Then they came to their senses and realised that it was about time they went home, because the bombing had stopped.

...

The other thing that happened when the war came was that the population of San Ginese tripled overnight. The retreating German army scattered across the breadth of the Italian peninsula and formed six columns, one of which travelled along the statale road that ran past the bottom of the Speranza hill and through San Leonardo, as Bucchione had predicted. But because they had dispersed to avoid casualties from the aerial bombardments, thousands of Germans abandoned the main roads and wandered around the countryside.

The Germans had already taken away the men who were healthy and strong to work in their factories, and were now seizing farm produce and livestock. As well as the cows and the pigs, they took horses. The war was clearly not going well if they needed horses to carry their great war machine. Or perhaps they just ate them.

After two German soldiers were killed by Italian *partigiani* in nearby Padule di Fucecchio, the Germans had massacred all the people in the town, most of them women and children. News of this evil act quickly circulated through the district and reached San Ginese, where people were so terrified that they bowed their heads and looked at their feet and shuffled about pretending they'd heard nothing.

Then, when the Americans broke through the enemy line along the Arno River, the German army, including the unit from Padule di Fucecchio, withdrew into the Garfagnana hills, where it formed what came to be known as the Gothic Line. As the Germans ran away, thousands of them passed through San Ginese.

The Enchanted Glade and the Babbling Brook

It was during this retreat that a German *Unteroffizier* one afternoon strolled through the gap between Vitale's stable and Edda's house and into the Mattei Courtyard. He stood in the middle of the yard and called out: '*Achtung! Achtung! Italiani contadini!*'

First he looked inside the stable and then he kicked open the kitchen door, splintering the jamb and scattering pieces of the latch across the mottled stone floor.

Irma stepped timidly out into the late afternoon sunlight, squinting behind her thick spectacles and wiping her hands on her apron. She was confronted by a man in a field-grey uniform and ankle-high shoes with gaiters (leather was scarce and they had run out of boots).

The man was shouting at her in broken Italian: '*Tu portare vacca piazza chiesa domani ore sette!* You to take cow church square tomorrow seven o'clock morning!'

And then he named the town where the massacre had taken place, to concentrate her mind in case she was wondering whether to comply.

He extracted a pencil from his top pocket, scribbled on a scrap of paper, threw it at Irma's feet and wrote something in a notebook. '*Capito, tu porca contadina?* Understand, you peasant sow?'

Irma nodded, blindly, behind her large round lenses, staring sideways at the ground and the piece of paper, avoiding eye contact with the loud, angry man who frightened her.

Her son Bruno, known as Succhio, also known as the Sucker of the Flat Thumb, was hiding behind the woodpile and ready to leap on the soldier with an axe when Vitale slapped a big calloused hand over his son's mouth and glared at him with wide eyes and lips drawn tautly over toothless gums, frightening the life out of him. Sucker's nostrils flared and he glared back but settled down.

They heard the German's shoes turn in the gravel and the fading *crunch crunch crunch*. He was gone. Both men came out.

'That cow is not going to the church tomorrow, ma.'

'If I don't take it to them, they'll come for it and then there'll be trouble for us. He wrote it all down – see, number eighty-seven. That's the cow and the place, our stable.'

Sucker was headstrong and volatile. To avoid military service and fighting on the German side under the fascists he had joined the military police. Even then, at the first opportunity he had jumped off the back of a truck carrying new recruits to their training camp and run away to hide in the hills.

...

The morning after the German's visit, Sucker refused to let his mother take the cow to the muster. He had decided on a course of action and he persuaded Vitale, the man who'd been to California and worked with Percheron horses, and his mother, who had introduced the blood of tall men to the family, to help him. Irma sent young Ugo up to the church to fetch the priest for a funeral to be held later that day.

Sitting at a table in the church square, next to the memorial to the fallen of the Great War, the German drew a line through the items in his inventory as each was delivered: cows, pigs, sacks of corn and flour, wheels of cheese and demijohns of wine, into which the villagers had poured just enough vinegar to make the wine turn after a few days.

When he'd finished, there remained just one item without a line through it. He remembered number eighty-seven: the brown cow with the spotted udder owned by the big half-blind woman with the broken veins on her red cheeks from drinking too much wine. Unteroffizier Hermann Gebauer pushed his chair back from the table in the gravel of the piazza, adjusted the holster of his Luger and strode off down the hill, followed at a safe distance by Don Mori and Little Ugo. Lida heard someone crashing through the scrub, saw the German walk past and sounded the alarm.

Sucker, who had been waiting all morning, leaned against the stable door next to the kitchen. He was starting to think the German had forgotten about their cow, and was almost annoyed about missing out on a fight, but when he heard Lida's voice calling out 'Pasquale! Pasquale!' he knew the enemy was on his way. If she had called out 'Pasquale, Giovanni!' he would have known there was more than one.

As Hermann tramped purposefully towards the yard, his killer heard him coming and stepped out from behind the corner of the stable. Sucker had already started swinging, so that as he moved out into the open the weapon was halfway through its trajectory. The shovel he used to pile manure and straw onto the compost heap struck his victim squarely on the forehead, knocking him out. Sucker cried, '*Pezzo di merda!*' The father leapt out from behind the son, the second wave of the planned attack, and with one thrust of the pitchfork skewered the

unconscious German where he lay in the dirt, ruining his uniform and inflicting ugly chest wounds. The tines of the fork, buried deep in the chest and twisted savagely, lacerated Hermann's heart and tore apart his lungs. A large jet of blood gushed from a severed artery, collected underneath his jacket and seeped into the courtyard.

The two stripped the uniform from the body while Irma removed the square wooden cover from the cesspit. Don Mori, who had arrived in time to see the soldier felled, read the burial rite as Sucker and Vitale slid the naked body into the slightly acrid, sweet-smelling brown liquid. Sucker poured a sack of lime on the corpse to help it on its way home to the god of dead Nazis and the butchers of civilians.

Irma cut the uniform – jacket, shirt, breeches, singlet and underpants – into a thousand small pieces and fed them to the blazing fire in the kitchen under the soot-coated soup cauldron. While Vitale removed all signs of blood from the yard, Sucker helped his mother with the shoes, sawing them in two and then four. They worked quietly and contentedly. The fire burnt brighter for an hour or two, and by the time they finished, the black cabbage soup was ready.

...

The Enchanted Glade and the Babbling Brook

Something else happened the day Sirio lost his legs and his member and then died. The same thing that happened every time the Americans and the Germans threw bombs across the sky at each other.

As the artillery shells shrieked overhead, in the dark recesses of the cave under Lilì's place, where half the village hid, you could hear murmuring and occasionally a squeal of delight or a moan, followed by barely audible gasps and rapid, accelerating intakes of breath.

Some women preferred to squat while others lay flat on their backs, with their legs apart as if they were giving birth. It seemed to everyone quite fitting that women should conceive while adopting the same posture in which they delivered, although there was no conceiving here, except in circumstances where one or both parties lost control of their wits.

Michelino's son Alfredo one day went too far and tried to substitute his proper part for the usual middle finger and Bruna slapped him on the side of the head, landing an enormous blow to the temple that temporarily rendered him unconscious. They delivered him to his mother with his member hanging out and still erect. The poor woman cried out to God, begging forgiveness for her reprobate son, and fainted on the floor beside him.

So, whenever the bombing started and the general alert went out, the lonely war wives in particular made sure they were first into the cave to occupy the space at the back. They took up their positions, naked under their skirts, open to most kinds of propositions in the dark. The aroma of warm water and corn meal wafted about the cave, and when the others noticed it they knew what was going on and became quiet and respectful, as if they were all participating in some kind of sacred rite. While at one end of the cave the members of the audience touched index fingers to closed lips and lifted their eyebrows, at the other end, the darker end, skirts were raised and rustled. Leather soles scraped on loose pebbles as the squatting women tried to keep their balance and give the boys room to manoeuvre. It was only the boys who took part, because the wives kept a close watch on their husbands, usually by holding on tight to their belts so they couldn't wander away.

After each bombardment, the floor of the cave was marked with small round patches of moisture and the whole place smelled like a steaming pot of fresh polenta.

And another thing that happened that day inside the cave, as the boys and the women laboured away, was that an idea started to grow inside Bucchione's head, a bright little diamond in his brain. He was starting to recover from the humiliation of his failed prediction.

He wasn't going to make any pronouncements this time, though. He would just talk to himself until he'd worked out what to do. The villagers could please themselves.

'Sirio has been badly hurt. He'll soon be dead. His poor mother and father and brother have wrapped his bleeding stumps in bed linen and are pouring wine down his throat to try to replace his blood.'

Sometimes he said the words out loud, forgetting that he was talking to himself. This time, Beo, who was always nearby, heard him.

'The war is becoming serious. We're caught in the crossfire between two fronts, the Germans at Castello and the Americans on the Montanari hill. We need to get behind one of the fronts and stay there, until both armies have moved on. Consider the American front. There's nowhere to go behind the American front, just the flat plain of Lucca. If I take my family out of here, it's best if we go behind the German lines, up into the hills of Compito, to the old mill. Listen to me' – he addressed himself directly now, as if to convince himself – 'I have pretended to be sick so I could avoid military service for this bastard regime and not be sent to the Russian front. I wanted to look after my family. I am not going to have them die in this shithole from a stray American bomb. Do you hear me?'

For now that was as far as Bucchione's thinking went, because the armies had finished shooting at each other for the day and suddenly there was a silence so vast and thick it filled all the world's empty space. If you sat still and held your breath for a moment, you could hear it. The only earthly sound came from the back of the cave, where Bruna was howling and banging the ground with her fists, raising a cloud of dust that drifted towards the entrance and made the others cough as they sat huddled together. She was always the noisiest, and as usual sounded either ecstatic or upset about something, but nobody had the courage to walk over to see if she was alright. She cried out one last time with all the strength she could muster from her lungs and her vocal chords, let out an enormous groan and either died or immediately fell asleep. You could hear the silence of the absent bombs again.

Beo crept out through a narrow gap between the rocks covering the entrance and climbed up alongside the house to the Beàno courtyard.

Soon they heard him calling the all-clear. '*Venite gente! Qui han finito!* Come out! They've finished out here!'

The women, including Bruna, who had woken up, tidied themselves, slipped their shoes back on, wiped their parts and adjusted their aprons. The boys made complaining noises, mumbled something about not having finished yet and sniffed their fingers appreciatively. Then everyone crawled stiffly out into the open air, stretched, yawned, looked up at the sky to make sure there were no more bombs coming, and wandered home.

...

In the night German troop carriers and tanks rolled through the village, gouging holes in the road with their metal tracks when they spun around on the spot. A truck knocked a large piece of stone and mortar from the corner of Vitale's wine cellar. For days the convoy rumbled past, raising dust and scattering stones and wearing a ditch on the inside of the bend in front of Gino's house, just under the lamppost, and another near Lida's place.

The cannons had gone quiet and the convoy kept coming. It was clear that some kind of retreat had started, but there was one more series of explosions left.

It came in the middle of the next night, from the Porcari side, to the east, beyond the Baracca tavern. Bucchione heard it and guessed what they were doing. The retreating Germans were blowing up the retaining walls of the Rogio irrigation channel and releasing the water into the low-lying land the villagers called *padule*, the swamp, although there had been no water in it for twenty years. Now, you must understand that the regular word for swamp is *palude* (not *padule*) but the local population, preferring to avoid having soft consonants and vowels succeed each other, which requires the tongue to perform acrobatics (albeit gentle ones in this case), arranged things so that the harder consonant came before the vowel. So *palude* became *padule* and was thereafter easier to pronounce. In any case, Bucchione cursed the Nazis, the fascists and the whores who were their mothers who gave birth to them.

By morning the water from the Rogio had flooded the plain that Mussolini had drained, in the days when he made the trains punctual and performed other administrative miracles. The water covered Monkey's Field, which Vitale had bought with his American money and would later give to Sucker to build a house on, after Sucker came back from Australia. With the return of the water, it was like in the olden days, when Villora was perched on the edge of a malarial swamp where mosquitoes swarmed and children died like flies.

The Enchanted Glade and the Babbling Brook

Ugo and Gino took a boat out onto the newly formed lake to catch frogs. They looked in the long grass near the embankment where the small brown jumping things would have sought refuge as the waters rose. Gino carried a long pole, one end of which he thrust into the grass. Then he twisted it. And twisted it and twisted it. As he twisted, the grass tore and wrapped itself around the bottom of the pole, forming a large ball. He raised the pole up to the sky and let it fall so the end hit the ground hard. Dozens of frogs fell out, and Ugo leapt from the boat and scrambled about to catch them and throw them in a hessian sack.

After dipping the only edible part, the legs, in egg and coating them in flour seasoned with salt and pepper, Irma fried them in oil and the entire family feasted on the newly flooded Monkey's Field frogs' legs.

...

A few days after the last of the trucks had trundled through, on the day Sucker killed the soldier, the krauts who had stayed back sent out a small search party. At the same time, the Americans scored a direct hit on the German artillery unit at Castello, and in the chaos no-one really missed Unteroffizier Hermann Gebauer, whom they assumed had either been blown to pieces or had run away with some plump, soft, rosy-cheeked peasant girl – the war was not going well, and no-one begrudged him that. Still, the Germans had to make a fuss, so they trooped half-heartedly about Villora, smashing doors and knocking people over, looking in cellars and attics in case Hermann had been kidnapped, and stealing any food and wine they hadn't already taken.

This went on for a whole day and caused commotion in the village. People hid in cellars and in every hole they could find and, if discovered, peered out at their oppressors with large, pleading eyes.

That was it. Bucchione's mind was made up. He told his family that night. 'Family,' he said, 'it's time to go.'

Little Morena skipped out into the courtyard straightaway to tell her little friends. Her little friends wanted to go too so they ran home to tell their mothers and fathers: 'Can we go too? Can we go too?'

When their parents heard what Bucchione was up to, the fact that he hadn't said anything to them about his plans made them suspicious. What did he know that he wasn't telling them? On the other hand, he'd been wrong before. The danger seemed to have passed. The convoy proved that the Germans were running away. They had only left a small artillery battery at Castello to slow the American pursuit. Of course, a few of them had come to the village and stormed around making a lot of noise, yet they hadn't really hurt anyone and had left, and everything was quiet now.

But then the Sanginesini started to think about how clever and strong and determined Bucchione was, how he had defied the attempts by the local recruitment office to send him to the Russian front to die or lose his fingers and toes to frostbite.

The people of the village wondered what he was thinking about. They knew that he had a fanatical devotion to his poor wife, Iose the Flour-Eater, his two children and his mother and father and unmarried sister Gemma, and would never let anything happen to them. If he was going to take them away from the village, he must have a good reason. And then Beo told them what Bucchione had said to himself in the cave, especially the part about loved ones dying in a shithole.

By morning all one hundred and twenty villagers had looked one another in the eye and decided they weren't going to miss out, whatever happened. They would go too.

...

On Sundays, as God had ordained they should after a hard week's fighting, both warring armies slept late and then attended their battlefield Mass.

At sunrise, the Villoresi said goodbye to their cows, pigs, rabbits and chickens. With the help of Julio the Orphan, the animals would fend for themselves until the villagers returned. Julio would sacrifice his safety to stay behind and look after them, for a small consideration.

Julio was a single man who wore thick glasses, without which he had almost no physical presence in the village. 'Oh, you mean the one with the thick glasses,' people would say.

He was an orphan, but his lack of parents seemed especially significant because his sisters had also died and he had no wife, no betrothed and no friends. It was as if every human being on earth had died and left him bereft, the most orphaned of orphans. In fact, people often forgot he lived in the village, and if they ran into him in the street they wondered who he was. He worked hard and kept to himself and almost never spoke. Whenever he did open his mouth to say something, he made self-deprecating statements that managed to appear high-sounding and not at all practical, so people thought of him as something of a philosopher, although this didn't seem to make much sense given he did nothing but shovel cow shit out of his stables all day. He had been saying he wanted to emigrate to Argentina, not California, where everyone else was going.

If you asked him how he was, you might almost regret it because he would start talking and sound as if he would never stop, and just by way of a beginning he would say: 'How do you expect me to be? I'm as well as can be expected. I expect you would understand, though, if you consider that I am an orphan and that both my sisters have died and that I have no fields but only my stables. Still, there's no point feeling sorry for me. We are put on this earth to live our lives and to get through each day until the one who put us here removes us from it. Meanwhile, we must do our duty and our work and take what satisfaction we can from our daily travails. It seems to me this is a truth universally acknowledged.'

So when he heard the others were leaving for a safe location to await the passing of the war, he prepared a short speech, and delivered it standing on the wall on the bend, under the village's only streetlight, in front of Gino's place.

'I'm a single man,' he told them, wearing the large, dirty brown overcoat covered in oily stains he wore all year round. 'I wear glasses with lenses as thick as the bottoms of bottles, and no woman will ever want me. When I look at a woman I have to get so close to her with my nose that my large eyeballs frighten her. My parents and my sisters are dead. No-one will miss me if I am blown to bits. But if I survive, I tell you now, I will emigrate to Argentina, the silver land, named after a refined, elegant, precious metal, not the garish gold of El Dorado, where many of our townspeople perished or whence they returned, but only after losing their hearts and their minds. My mind is made up. Don't try to stop me.'

They all had to acknowledge that he was right. No-one would miss him. And no-one tried to stop him. He stayed behind and did the rounds of the stables, the pigsties, the chicken coops and the rabbit hutches. And later, after it was all over, he sailed to Argentina wearing a new brown overcoat he'd bought with the money the villagers paid him, and new thick lenses in shiny new frames.

The Enchanted Glade and
the Babbling Brook

Bucchione strolled out of *casa vecchia*, the old family home, closely followed by Iose the Flour-Eater, his unmarried sister Gemma, little Morena and little Paolo, his mother Teresa and his father Paolino, who kept muttering, '*Tutti i popoli! Tutti i popoli!* All the peoples! All the peoples!' They carried only a few items of clothing rolled up in two bundles, and some food: bread and cheese, half a prosciutto, a flask of wine, two flasks of water and three light but cumbersome sacks filled with corn husks to serve as mattresses.

Morena held old Paolino firmly by the hand. She was making sure he wasn't left behind, which had happened once before when they had all fled to the bomb shelter under Villora. It was Morena who ran back into the house to get her sweet old grandfather and found him by the fire, sounding demented. '*Tutti i popoli! Tutti i popoli!*' he was crying.

As they marched out, the rest of the village was waiting, each family queued in a line behind its half-opened front door – father, mother, children. Thirty metres along, and the whole of Beàno was behind them. At Il Sasso, another thirty villagers joined in. Those who lived at the Houses Above, and in the Mattei Courtyard,

Canaponi and the Winds, waited by the side of the road and, as the procession passed, took their turn at stepping into the line. By the time they reached Monkey's Field, where Ugo and Gino's boat was moored, all one hundred and twenty had fallen in behind Bucchione, who was striding ahead, cigar firmly stuck inside his left cheek, straw-strewn greasy sweat-stained hat askew, not quite Moses but almost, arms swinging, humming 'The Internationale' quietly to himself. He didn't want the others to hear, especially the Catholics, who were good people but misguided. If they heard the communist anthem they might cause a ruckus, and that would not be good.

Bucchione had decided they would go to Ponte alle Corti in Compito, a village one long day's walk away, deep in a valley between heavily forested mountains that offered protection on all sides – a place unlikely to be caught in the crossfire between batteries launching bombs at each other.

The Enchanted Glade and the Babbling Brook

He described the place to those who came up and walked alongside him for a while. The scene he depicted caused his companions to be overcome by a frenzied kind of joy. Beo, who was highly strung and excitable anyway, ran into the bushes on the side of the road to relieve himself.

What awaited them, Bucchione said, was an Enchanted Glade ('Of course, glades are always enchanted,' they said as they nodded and clapped) hidden under ancient plane trees, whose highest branches formed a protective canopy where at night the flickering fireflies of autumn glided among the bushes. They would set up camp inside the ancient mill, beside which flowed a babbling brook ('Of course, brooks are always babbling,' they cheered). Bucchione, having noticed their agitation, decided there and then to stop describing their destination lest they become nervous wrecks. He sighed loudly to show them he had finished and chewed harder on his cigar.

The line of marchers skirted the newly flooded swamp along the edge of the San Ginese hill. It was a cool, cloudless autumn morning, with a suggestion of the final warmth of summer to return later that day. There was in the air a stillness that crept up and made you scan the horizon and turn around suddenly to look behind you.

Since the start of the war San Ginese had become a very quiet place, apart from the explosions, and fear made people hold their breath as they listened for approaching bombs. They all walked around as quiet as mice, as the saying goes, heads bowed, looking at their feet, whispering. At Il Porto they strode past Folaino's house and everyone turned to look, although of course he was long gone, dead and buried. Then they looked at Tommaso, who had fired four American bullets into Folaino's chest from a Smith & Wesson Model 10 double-action revolver, bought in Manhattan, killing him immediately. Tommaso the Killer stared straight ahead and shuffled along, head swaying from side to side.

...

One more kilometre down the road and they were in Centoni, the ancestral home of Bucchione's wife, Iose the Flour-Eater, and here they stopped to rest in the large courtyard behind the house of her father and mother, Giuseppe Dal Porto and Carolina Luporini, who lived there with Iose's sad brother Derì and mysterious sister Fulvia. Iose the Flour-Eater ran to embrace her mother, Carolina.

The group slowly disintegrated as people staggered and stopped, stooped, milled around, and then fell flat on their backs as if shot, stretched out on the ground, or sat on the low stone wall that separated the house from a vineyard. The men scratched themselves here and there, as did the less elegant women. The children chased one another behind the outhouses and among the vines, shrieking and laughing and tumbling around on the grass.

Vitale, like many men, only washed himself when the water ran freely in the irrigation ditches, after the sluice gate had been opened by some local official at certain times of the growing season. Usually he washed himself like a cat would. When the irrigation water was released, though, he would jump in, bare-chested and trouser-less, and throw water on his important bits, meaning his armpits, chest, neck, face and head, and scrub everything between his legs, the front and the back. It was quite a scene when suddenly all the men in the fields were standing in water up to their waists, removing clothes, splashing, rubbing various body parts frantically, gasping at the cold and shouting at one another like playful children. This cleansing went on for at least three minutes, after which they considered themselves clean enough to last until the next time.

But there hadn't been any water in the ditches for several months and Vitale, who had worn the same clothes for a long time, stank.

He unrolled a trouser cuff and three pieces of shrapnel tumbled onto the ground. Normally a quiet, unassuming man, he became animated when he showed the jagged bits of metal proudly to anyone who revealed the slightest interest, putting them back and pulling them out repeatedly and making sure you knew how close he had come to having his leg blown off and even being killed. Everyone marvelled at how fortunate he was. Beo, who was jealous of the attention, said Vitale had put the bits of metal in there himself so he would have something to talk about and appear more interesting than he was. He waved his hand dismissively and looked away while rolling his eyes and saying, 'Bah!'

At Centoni urns of water and flasks of light red wine did the rounds, wheels of pecorino and caprino cheese were cut up, prosciutto was sliced, dried grapes and figs were distributed, loaves of bread were torn apart and devoured. It soon became a feast – not the wedding at Cana or the miracle of the loaves and fishes, but almost. There was no work to do that day, no prospect of any for at least a week. They had their families with them and they were being fed by friendly neighbours. What more could they want? And it was then that the ever-present thought in the back of every peasant's mind started to recede, until a few days later, in the depths of the Babbling Glade, or by the Enchanted Brook, it would disappear altogether.

...

They drank wine, Zena (who was Bulletta's brother) plucked a note or two on his mandolin, someone started singing and everyone joined in. The favourable movement of the air and the conformation of the landscape carried the song as far as the church on the hill.

They sang 'Lo Spazzacamino', that well-known song about a wandering chimney sweep who visits a widow, eats well and drinks his fill, and then goes up the hole, the hole in her chimney, which she shows him. She expresses her worry that her chimney is narrow and feels sorry for him that he may not be able to go up. He reassures her that he is an expert and has been at it for many years and knows how to do his duty and will have no trouble going up. The song goes on about the sweep going up the black hole and managing to squeeze in quite easily and being good at it and in fact quite expert, and ends with the expression of the widow's gratitude for the chimney sweep's skill. Four months later, of course, there is a large crescent moon, and not just in the sky, and five months after that a beautiful baby boy is born, who all the villagers can see is the spit and image of the chimney sweep.

This song, sung by a choir of one hundred and twenty exiles, echoed around the hills and through the nearby hamlets like some heavenly hallucination for the ears.

When they finished singing, they all fell asleep, and by the time they awoke three hours later they realised they would have to hurry to reach Compito before nightfall. Reluctantly they got to their feet.

Fifty metres down the road, once they had reached the outskirts of Centoni, they left the foothills of San Ginese behind and struck out across a narrow strip of flat land alongside a tobacco field for a few kilometres, passed the disused railway station whose roof had caved in, and headed for the Compito crossroads, to the butcher's shop on one side and the police station, where Tommaso the Killer had been locked up temporarily, on the other.

At the crossroads they turned right and started to climb, the road winding its way up the sunny eastern side of the Compito hill, through terraced olive groves and vineyards. It was a Sunday so there was no-one about. The locals were asleep in their houses.

In the olden days Compito had the biggest church, presided over by the Head Priest of the district, so naturally it was where criminals were decapitated. A cage, hanging on a rusty chain from a pole that protruded through an arch at the top of the church's belltower, swung slowly in the wind. The chain creaked as the cage swayed left and right while slowly spinning clockwise, then swayed right and left while spinning back the other way. In the cage they had once put heads that had been removed from their owners' bodies in the piazza below, a warning to potential miscreants, malefactors and wrongdoers.

The sun was about to set and the exhausted villagers were staggering backwards and forwards and from one side of the road to the other. They felt the burden of the day's walk, especially after eating and drinking so much at Centoni. Occasionally someone in the column would drop to his knees and bend forwards to rest his forehead on the ground, and would be frozen until someone else delivered him a solid kick in the backside and made him jump up and stumble back into the line.

Bucchione stopped in the middle of the road and waited. He seemed to be getting his bearings. Those immediately behind him walked into one another and toppled over, falling like dominoes, until eventually those at the back caught on and also stopped. The cage dangling high above their heads creaked again ominously. The path turned behind the tower and started to drop away quickly down the hill on the other side, then levelled out and continued running beside the Visona, which, now in full flow, was a torrent of thundering, boiling water, tumbling tree trunks, crashing branches and rolling rocks. They had found the Babbling Brook.

The pause seemed to give them all new vigour, enough at least for one final effort.

Bucchione moved off and they followed him through a natural archway formed by two monstrous plane trees growing a metre apart. In they went, single file, the men of each family group first, to make sure it was safe. It was like a giant's lair under a canopy of ancient trees. Beo could have sworn one leafy colossus spoke to him in a deep breathy whisper: 'Welcome, skinny toothless man.' Leaping out of his skin, he spun around in a circle, surveying the territory. But there was nothing there.

They had found the Enchanted Glade.

Centenarian trees on each side of the torrent had made a roof where their high branches fused, up near the clouds. At first it was dark in the giant's green house, but soon their eyes became accustomed to the dappled light (yes, light is always dappled in such places). The plane trees would normally be bare by now, but there were just a few leaves scattered about.

The mill-house, its large wheel broken, lay abandoned, dusty and empty, like the villagers themselves, who were tired, grey and hollowed out from their journey. This would be their home for now. Once they had seen it was safe, the men called their families into the Enchanted Glade.

The Sanginesini dispersed inside the derelict stone building, staking out little family plots, smoothing out their sacks of corn husks to lie on and rest aching bones. A few made a mattress out of their husband or father, who lay down on the ground with his wife and children and elderly parents on top of him, so that here and there dotted about the large room were small piles of people, chests and breasts rising and falling, breathing, snoring gently. The Sanginesini had three major aims in life: to work, eat and sleep with the people they loved. Although the work was suspended, their other desires were fulfilled.

The local villagers brought in great cauldrons of bean soup to feed them all and woke them up. But after the feast at Centoni no-one was very hungry.

In the bushes the fireflies glided about.

The Enchanted Glade and the Babbling Brook

...

On the first day the sun got up late and so did the cavernicolous villagers, who moped around not knowing what to do with themselves now that they were away from their fields and their stables. Some even felt nostalgic for the exploding bombs; when Beo dared to say this Bucchione almost whacked him with the back of his hand, which he raised but left suspended in midair.

Only Argante, who came from the hamlet of Cecchini, on the rise above the Speranza hill crossroads, fell into his usual routine, which was to sound the alarm. Argante was highly respected among his extended family and gave himself airs, but everyone else thought he was mad. He claimed he could hear American bomber squadrons taking off from the airfield that the Allies had built more than one thousand kilometres away, in Malta.

At six o'clock in the morning he leapt into the centre of the large communal bedroom inside the mill and, his legs wide apart, arms raised, palms open, eyeballs protruding, he cried out: '*Ragazzi, scappiamo, gli aerei son partiti!* Everybody, run – the planes have taken off!'

They all ignored him and someone threw a shoe, telling him to go back to sleep.

The hours passed and they wandered about listlessly or slept and farted in their sleep as the beans from the night before worked their way through their intestines. For the midday meal the Compitesi brought them wooden platters piled high with slices of *farinata*, a polenta made from a thick soup of white beans, black Tuscan cabbage, carrots, celery and pigs' trotters. They roasted the slices over open fires to make a crisp crust on the outside, leaving a warm softness inside, sweet with the beans and cabbage. On the roasted slices they sprinkled spicy olive oil.

The Compitese wine was made from the grapes grown in the terraced vineyards they had passed on their way up the hill. It was mellow and friendly, but not too sweet. Even the children drank a splash with their water.

Very soon after the midday meal all the Sanginesini were fast asleep again. They slumbered all afternoon and only stirred as the sun fell behind the mountain and the dappled light lost its dapple and the warmth left the world. They then lit fires and huddled around wrapped in blankets, telling stories about America and the men and women who had gone there and come back, including Tommaso, who on request stood and bowed and recited the famous words: 'Your Honour, I did my duty. Nothing more, nothing less.'

And naturally everyone roared their approval, laughing and cheering and clapping like excited children.

The occasional explosion could be heard in the distance, but the time that elapsed between one bomb and the next grew longer and longer, so that by the end of the day they had almost forgotten there was a war outside the Enchanted Glade.

Late in the day, Bucchione and a few helpers cleared some of the bushes away from the windows of the mill to let in more light. Bucchione was restless.

Then, in the tradition of the *veglia*, which is a time when people stay awake together by the fire or, if the weather allows, in the courtyard, to talk and keep one another company, Bulletta told the story of Il Sasso, the foundation stone for what became Gino's house on the bend, near the single lamppost.

The Compitesi, who were less gregarious than the Sanginesini, shyly gathered around, after asking for permission to listen in.

. . .

'So, I will tell you about Il Sasso.

'Beàno is a fragment of Villora, a lane about fifty metres long, which extends from Gino's house on the corner past half a dozen houses to the courtyard in front of Bucchione's house. In Beàno now live Lilì and her husband, Il Moro, with their sons Giovanni and Rinaldo, who are two really big boys, and Claudio Andolfi and his mother, Giraldina; his father, Ricciardo; and his brother, Vittorio, who is always scolding Claudio for not doing his schoolwork. Giraldina has large circles around her eyes and a beaklike nose that make her look like a benevolent owl. Two widowed sisters who dress in black live in the first house on the left and ride their cow-drawn cart everywhere. Next to Lilì lives Bucchione and his family, and we all know them. These are all good people.

'So, this fragment of the village is known as Beàno and no-one can remember why. The village was already called Villora and its houses were not numbered and the one proper street that passed through it was nameless.

'Anyway, one end of Beàno later became known as Il Sasso. In Beàno, on Gino's land, along the line of the garden wall, where the single lamppost is now, stood a large truncated pyramid-shaped stone. It was a feature of the village and the locals were proud of it, and possessive of it, in the same way some cities in Italy are proud of the relics of a saint, like the relics of Saint Mark the Evangelist in St Mark's Basilica in Venice.

'The stone had earlier been cemented in place so that no-one could move it, because despite its enormous weight it had once been stolen. This is how it happened.

In the old days the rivalry of the scattered hamlets in the village of San Ginese led to fist fights among gangs of young men. They also played pranks of epic proportions on one another.

'One night, after there had been several physical encounters in the courtyards and streets over some insult one ruffian had uttered about the alleged lost virginity of another's sister, the Cimaioli, who were from Lecci and Collina, stole the large stone from the Villoresi and dropped it down a dry well near the church at the top of the San Ginese hill. The Cimaioli did not try to hide the fact they had done it but boasted of their superiority and dared the Villoresi to retrieve the monolith.

'It was again at night a week later that ten young Villoresi trooped off up to the well, carrying ropes and pulleys and long wooden poles. They tied one end of a rope to a tree, and Gino and Palle slid down into the well, landing in shallow mud. They used a broken wagon shaft as a lever to raise the boulder a few centimetres on one side so they could slip a rope loop under it. Then they repeated this with another rope on the other side. For good measure they strapped a third loop horizontally around the lower half, and then they climbed out. With the ropes threaded through large pulleys tied to a strong timber beam, the ten hauled half the night, lifting the boulder in its improvised sling a little at a time until it was freed from its damp prison.

'They rolled the stone downhill to Villora in fits and starts, using a wooden beam as a brake. This was in late June, and tiny fireflies danced around them, lighting the way, while a large friendly moon smiled down on the party. The young men of Villora had won the contest, and pride had been restored to the village.'

The entire population of the mill exploded, cheering and applauding, even the Compitesi, who had by now practically become naturalised Sanginesini.

'On the corner where the haystack and the old stables were, that later became Gino's place, they dug a hole and half buried the stone, pouring concrete around it to hold it in place.

'There it remained until Gino smashed it to pieces to build the foundations of his house. That part of Villora soon had a new name so that what was once the far end of Beàno became Il Sasso, and that is what it is to this day.'

A loud sigh filled the air, followed by some yawns, then more yawns, then some mumbles and a general hubbub of people talking about the weight of the stone, the size of the ropes, the names of the young men involved. Everyone felt satisfied because Bulletta had told the story well, and they felt renewed pride in their village.

The little children with big round eyes and wide open ears had been hiding between the legs of the grown-ups as they listened to the story. Now their mothers and fathers told them to go to bed. 'Hey, you! What are you doing there? Go to bed. It's dark and it's late.'

The Compitesi said goodnight and went to their houses, through the archway, outside the Enchanted Glade.

So the sun came up and went down again.

...

On the second day they slept until midday again. It now looked as if this would be the new pattern of life. When they were all awake and fed, Bucchione got some men to help him fix the roof of the mill house. This was the first work anyone had done for a while and it gave them satisfaction.

Bucchione felt a desire to sow some vegetables suited to the time of year, so he made a list using the lead pencil and notebook he always carried: spinach, onions, lettuce, beetroot, radish, onions, carrots, cabbage, rocket, leeks, valerian, chicory, radicchio, endive and pink garlic. Alternatively, he could transplant garlic, onions, cauliflower, fennel, lettuce, chives, laurel, oregano, sage, thyme, mint and rosemary.

The Compitesi, he was sure, would either provide the seeds or a few small plants. There was ample water from the Babbling Brook. All he needed to start a vegetable garden in the Enchanted Glade was a slightly sunny spot that provided plenty of protection from the extreme cold. It was still too early to make a decision about this, though. They had walked out of San Ginese thinking they might be absent for a week, but no-one knew what the war would bring. So he would wait.

Beo ran back down the hill to the police station at the crossroads to ask if the two warring armies had passed, but the *carabinieri* said they hadn't seen anyone or anything that looked like an army, let alone two. It was too soon to return home. The German artillery post was still entrenched at Castello, near the church, and the Americans were still on the Montanari hill. In fact, there were three explosions that day that came from the direction of San Ginese.

After some initial discomfort, many of the villagers were becoming used to their new life. The men sat and played *briscola* and *scopa*, slapping cards down on the table defiantly with exclamations of jubilant victory: '*Toh!*' And the reply would come: '*Toh!*' Nara, the woman who was a man, smoked and played cards too. The feminine women chatted and the children played. Occasionally a fist fight would break out among the players over a hand of cards, but otherwise they were content and rested and certainly well-fed by the locals, who seemed to have an unending supply of food and wine. Even Argante had settled down and was no longer hearing aeroplanes in Malta.

Iose had persuaded one of the local women to give her a saucepan and a small bag of flour and to bring milk every morning. Iose the Flour-Eater sat in a dark corner of the cavernous mill in front of a wood stove stirring the flour into the milk to make a thick white sauce, into which she threw some olives. She rejoined the others only after she had eaten. In this way she tried to hide her eating perversion from the others, but they all knew anyway.

Small groups took to perambulating below the trees and along the torrent, venturing as far as the natural doorway they had crossed a few days before. They were afraid to venture outside, so turned their backs to the exit and marvelled at the beauty of their God-sent refuge and blessed Bucchione for having brought them there.

To pass the time, on the night of the second day Bucchione decided to tell the story of the stolen carts. Everybody had heard it before, but there is nothing as pleasurable as hearing a story you already know, especially if it is well told, and Bucchione was one of the best tellers of tales in San Ginese. Some of the Compitesi, who were boring people and very often bored, again joined the Sanginesini in their encampment and settled down to listen.

...

'Well, you all know how many years ago the young men of Villora stole the *barrocci* (the carts, from the Latin *birotium*, meaning two-wheeled), which were kept in the stables, and hid them. The first time they did this, it took everybody by surprise and no-one knew what was happening.

'It was on the eve of the May Day workers' holiday. In the middle of the night twenty *giovanotti* (young men) visited barns and stables in the village and took away some carts. It took three or four of these delinquents to push a cart all the way up the hill, so overall five carts disappeared. You can imagine how hard it is to push a cart weighing four or five quintals one kilometre up the San Ginese hill.

'To make it more interesting they took those that belonged to men who were most obviously proud of their carts, people like 'Nibale,

Enoè's son, whose stable is just past Lida's place on the way down to Sucker's. 'Nibale keeps his cart beautifully clean. All the metal bits are brightly polished and it has a nicely greased axle and shiny wheel hubs.

'He also has a whole philosophy of life based on the way a man keeps his cart. A man's attitude to his cart reveals a lot about him, according to 'Nibale. He says, "Tell me honestly, can you trust a man with a dirty cart? If your daughter wants to marry a man with a dilapidated cart, don't you think she had better think again? After all, if that's how he looks after his cart, then who knows what treatment he dishes out to the cows, who will be pulling the cart, and to his women? And you know the old saying – get your cows and your women from your own village only. Well, what about making sure you have a local cart, better still one made by a familiar tradesman, so you know where she's been and who with? Isn't that just as important? Did any good ever come of a man whose cart was poorly maintained? Beware a man with a shabby cart! That's what I say!"

"Nibale decorates his cows with red and gold pom poms on their noses. I have heard there are sacred cows in India that look like 'Nibale's cows! Merigon, that tall skinny type over there, on the other hand, is unlike 'Nibale in every way. His carts are always dirty and poorly maintained. 'Nibale cannot bear to see a cart that is mistreated like that, or to hear its squeaky wheel. When 'Nibale hears the cart with only one squeaky wheel passing his house, he runs out into the street waving his arms about, and stands in front of the cow and implores Merigon to let him lubricate the wheel. Merigon refuses. And while everyone else who has a cow hitched to a cart uses two ropes to guide her along – one rope to pull her to the left and one rope to pull her to the right – Merigon is so thrifty that he uses one rope only to turn her head in one direction and then the other. Consequently, the cow is always confused about which direction she is to turn in and often just walks in circles.

'Anyway, on the morning of the first of May, when the workers were marching in the cities all over the nation, the peasants of San Ginese got up at sunrise and went to work as usual. There was more than the usual bustle, though, out in the single street that runs straight through the heart of our village. The five *contadini* whose carts had disappeared, including 'Nibale, wandered around, forlornly leading their cows, halter ropes dangling limply; the men were bereft without their carts, stopping to ask other villagers, querying one another, knocking on doors, looking inside every stable in the village, standing stunned, blocking traffic, unable to comprehend what had happened.

'Suddenly, who arrives but Nilo, with his pants down around his ankles, struggling to keep them up as he runs through the crowd, breathless for more than one reason. He stops in the middle of the road and starts shouting at everyone to go and collect their carts, to get them out of there, because Father Palagi will be enraged. By the way' – here Bucchione broke character – 'why should that lazy vagabond of a priest be enraged about anything, given that he enjoys a blessed existence living off the fat of the land?'

The listeners nodded and he resumed the story.

'Well, Nilo said to 'Nibale and the other grief-stricken victims who had gathered in front of Gino's house on the corner, "You had better get your carts out of there because when the reverend wakes up and sees a fleet of wagons in the courtyard at the front of his church, he will censure the lot of you at Mass in front of everyone next Sunday, and might even excommunicate you!"

'His listeners heard this but it took some time for them to understand the meaning behind what he had said. They looked at Nilo and the pants he was holding up with both hands. Why was he losing his pants? What did the carts and the church have to do with Nilo's pants? They looked at him and they looked at one another.

'You see, Nilo had been up, so to speak ... up ... up ... for an all-night vigil! An all-night vigil with the *perpetua*, the priest's housekeeper, who is not so old as to be incapable and not so young as to object!'

The listeners roared their approval and several of them slapped Nilo on the back, leaving large bruises. One missed and struck him on the head, knocking him to the ground. He got up quickly and dusted himself down because he didn't want to miss the rest of the story in which he was a protagonist.

'There was no need to ask Nilo what he'd been up to. Everyone knew. They were just happy that their carts had turned up because *Nilo* had been up.'

The assembled audience cheered their approval and then arguments broke out among different factions about the merits or otherwise of 'Nibale's and Merigon's contrasting philosophies of the cart and Nilo's impure acts. The discussion kept them occupied for the rest of the evening. Nilo, Merigon and 'Nibale took it all in good humour. They were secretly delighted to be the protagonists of one of Bucchione's stories, even though he had decorated it a bit more than necessary.

So the sun came up and went down again.

...

On the third day Zena wondered aloud whether they couldn't just stay there forever. Then they spent several hours clearing the Babbling Brook of tree trunks and boulders. This improved the water flow, reduced the noise and made the raging torrent more like an actual babbling brook, although it had not been entirely tamed.

When Beo ran down the hill again for more information, the *carabinieri* told him that the last of the Germans had retreated during the night and the Americans had followed, so the danger was over and they could all go home. This was a shock. It took him an hour of wandering in circles outside the police station to gather his wits. Finally one of the beautifully uniformed officers pointed him back in the direction of Compito and gave him a shove.

When he reported back to the Sanginesini at the old mill, they became silent, stared at the ground, cleared their throats and kicked at the dirt floor until they all disappeared from view in a cloud of dust. This led to more throat-clearing.

They decided it was too soon for the fighting to be over, that the Germans couldn't possibly have left. The *carabinieri* clearly had it wrong. Maybe it was a few Germans from somewhere else and a small American patrol that had driven past. They decided it would be safer to wait.

As the sun began to set, Bucchione disappeared for a few hours. Morena and Paolo were hiding in a tree, his mother, Teresa, was busy tending to his demented father, his wife sat in her usual stultified fashion, staring into space, dreaming of béchamel sauce, and his sister Gemma was making sure everyone was happy. No one noticed he had gone.

The widow Pasquina's house was outside the glade and further down the hill, hidden in a copse of willows. All you had to do was stand outside her door and she would come out before you knocked and immediately ask you in, offering you a bowl of wine, which you gratefully accepted. You would drink several bowls and she would have a sip or two to keep you company. You told her whatever it was that was troubling you, as if she were a priest and this was a kind of confessional. Then she would strip you naked and take you to her bed.

Afterwards she filled a tub from a cauldron of water that was hanging from a chain above the fire and washed you, feeding you grapes, walnuts and goat's cheese as she poured hot water over your head and shoulders, easing from your limbs the painful weariness of your life. She was a rich widow and did not take payment for her services.

...

As the night of the third day approached, to relieve some of the boredom the children asked Beo to tell them the story of the *linchetto*, which they'd heard a thousand times before but of which they never tired. They asked Beo and not anyone else to tell the story because there was a suspicion that he was in fact a giant *linchetto* himself, skinny, jittery and skittish, with a pointed head. Beo enjoyed this small moment of fame and did nothing to persuade them he was not what their imaginations said he was.

This time, even the men and women gathered around the glow of thirty-two campfires, huddling with their children under blankets, prepared to hear once again a tale they always marvelled at. Once Beo had calmed down the crowd of noisy, wriggling children by threatening to call the *babào* to eat them, he began.

'*Ragazzi*, everyone knows that Genesius had a son who was called Tista. What is Tista short for?'

'Giovan Battista!' came the united cry, which they went on to repeat until it became a chant. 'Tista! Tista! Tista! Tista!'

'Shhh,' Beo hissed.

'Well, while Tista was in America, his wife Ancilla worked like a man and raised the children on her own – that is Vitale, who is over there, and his two sisters, who are hiding somewhere. She could work a field like her husband, hitching the same cow to the same plough and turning over hectares and hectares of soil. On long summer nights she would attach the cow to the *barroccio* and go to Verciano with little

Vitale and his two little sisters to visit relatives. They allowed her to fill a large wooden vat carried on the cart with brown liquid *perugino* from their cesspit. In Verciano, Ancilla filled the vat on the cart using a *getto*, a bucket with a long wooden handle, which she lowered into the cesspit to collect the brown liquid. By four o'clock in the morning she was back in the fields below Villora spreading the rich fertiliser, as her children slept under the driver's seat.'

At Beo's mention of sleep, some of the children yawned.

'One night on the way home in the dark, under a big August moon, they were wearily making their way along the bottom of the long, low hill at the end of which Villora sits, both a little perched upon, and a little submerged in, ancient moss and soft burial soil.' Beo said the words 'ancient moss and soft burial soil' in such a way that the children shrieked in surprise and fear.

'... As I was saying ... as they were going along *sottomonte*, which is the side of the San Ginese hill, Ancilla and the three children saw a green light dancing around, left and right and up and down, in the middle of the road. From a distance, except for the colour, it was a tongue of fire much like in the paintings of the Holy Spirit in the sacristy up at the church. As they came nearer they saw a little man, about thirty centimetres tall, who did not flinch but glared at them and suddenly charged at the cow in what seemed an attempt to frighten it. The cow took little notice, being used to these *linchetti*, who often pestered her and her companions in stables all over the Tuscan countryside. As you know, throughout the night peasants everywhere hear their animals complaining with moos and squawks and grunts ...'

'*Moo moo!*' shouted the children. A ripple like a soft wind on water ran through the crowd at the physical excitement of the children and the sighing of the happy watching parents.

'As we Tuscans know, the *linchetti*, those little pests, dart in and out of the straw and from behind wood stacks and piles of hay. The *contadini*, the farmers, know what is going on and aren't concerned, unless the noise from their stock becomes excessive. Then the farmer whose cow is heavy with calf or who has been poorly and down on her food will run to the stable for fear the animal will miscarry or get a fright and die.'

'Oooooh!' came the sound from the audience, halfway between a sigh and a moan.

'Having failed to excite the cow, the tiny goblin shot straight up in the air. Ancilla said it reminded her of the squirt of water at the village fountain whenever a mischievous boy stuck his index finger in the spout. The *linchetto* just as quickly descended, braked and landed softly on her head, where he sat with his legs crossed, ruffling her beautiful long black hair with his thin gnarled fingers. Vitale and his sisters cried and hid under a sack.'

Everyone looked for Vitale in the crowd and laughed, pointing their fingers at him, and if they were close enough they slapped him on the back and elbowed him in the ribs.

'Then, with one hand Ancilla held the cow's rope and, cursing her absent husband, with the other she took a swipe at the *linchetto* with her fist, which seemed to pass right through him. However, having achieved his purpose, which was to make a nuisance of himself, the green thing zigzagged away up the hillside, zoomed into the sky, paused, flipped over onto his head and dived into the earth, vanishing in the soft soil and leaving behind a puff of dust in the moonlight. His disappearance brought a magical stillness to the moonlit swamp and the familiar hills of San Ginese.'

'Aaaaahhh …' The children let out all the air they had been holding in their lungs.

'Later that day, after she had spread the *perugino* over the corn field and given the children their breakfast of sweet barley coffee and milk with bread, Ancilla told her husband Tista's parents, Genesius and Teresina, about the incident. Good Tuscan peasants that they were, they scarcely raised an eyebrow, and the rest of the village also took it in its stride, as word quickly spread among its one hundred and twenty inhabitants that while Tista was in America and Ancilla was having to do the work of a man, she and her three children had met a *linchetto* at the foot of the San Ginese hill on the way back from Verciano in the middle of the night, under a big August moon.'

Beo took a deep breath. The children yelped their approval, clapping and cheering, as did the mothers and fathers and everyone else, and pretty soon they were chanting, '*Ancora, ancora, ancora!*'

Beo took a bow.

Bucchione quietly read his list of vegetables to himself.

So the sun came up and went down again.

...

On the fourth day Bulletta, who was a storyteller, as you know, wondered aloud whether they couldn't just stay there forever.

'*Mah!*' he said.

And Zena replied, 'What does that mean, *mah*?'

Bulletta: 'When you are tired of living, you say *mah!*'

Zena: 'But only if you are very old and have seen so much that you have reached a point where you are confused, because your head is full to overflowing with all you have seen and you are unable to put it into any kind of order.'

Bulletta: '*Mah* means that you don't know anything anymore. That everything is as good or as bad as anything else. I am saying, we might as well stay here.'

Zena: 'But some people also say *ormai*. Which means, "What is the point? At this stage nothing matters anymore, it's too late."'

Bulletta: 'Exactly! Which is not so different from *mah!* In fact they are so close in meaning that for emphasis some people prefer to say, *Mah! Ormai!* That's what they would say if they were determined to stay here and never go back to San Ginese.'

A group was formed to discuss how this might be possible, but the conference encountered several major philosophical hurdles, and they decided to postpone the debate until further notice.

Everyone else woke up, ate and went back to sleep. Bucchione carefully studied the plans for his proposed vegetable garden.

So the sun came up and went down again.

...

On the fifth day Bulletta and Zena and a few of the other men went hunting for migratory birds flying south from Russia. The birds were looking for Africa, where the winter was not as harsh, but found the Sanginesini waiting with their double-barrelled shotguns instead. When migratory birds encountered fog or other bad weather on the Italian peninsula, they would veer right and approach Africa through Spain. Unfortunately there was no fog or other bad weather. The Italian autumn and winter that year were mild, so the birds flew straight over the hills of Compito, and the hunting group brought back eighteen thrushes, seven fieldfare (a type of thrush), eleven chaffinches, nine crows and twenty-four blackbirds, which were plucked, cleaned, hung up to mature, and roasted and eaten with polenta in a rich tomato condiment the next day.

If you study the taxonomy of birds, you realise how beautiful the Italian names of birds are. Here are just a few examples: *tordo* (a migratory bird, weighing less than 100 grams, light in colour), *merlo* (black, also weighs less than 100 grams), *cesena* (grey, weighs about 120 grams), *fringuello* (a colourful 20-gram combination of red and yellow), *cornacchia* (a 500-gram nasty pest of a bird).

As they were cleaning the birds, they teased one another.

'Sodo here, he's so economical he comes to Nedo's bar and sits and waits, doesn't order anything. Nedo goes over to him, wipes his table and asks him if he wants something to drink, and Sodo shakes his head. He's always waiting for someone to offer to buy him a coffee.'

Sodo threw a half-plucked crow at the speaker. 'What about you, Dolfo? Remember the potato seeds you brought back from America? You told us, "I sowed them in the terrace above and they sprouted in the terrace below." As if that is possible! You must have been drunk that day!'

Dolfo, who was from Cecchini, was sensitive to criticism of any kind. He was particularly thin-skinned about his marriage and the behaviour of his wife. She never helped him with any of the work in the fields. When he went out to load hay onto his cart, he would take a ladder with him. Other men had wives who would stand on top of the load and arrange the hay as the husband threw it up with a pitchfork. Dolfo would toss a few forkfuls of hay onto the cart and climb up the ladder to arrange the load. Then he would climb down, throw some hay up, climb the ladder again, and so on.

Next the group turned its attention to Treccia, who was described as a *trasandone*, which means he was a very untidy person. His wife, Giorgia, despaired. They laughed at him because he loved lying in bed and would go to bed wearing his stable clothes. He said whoever had invented the bed should be given a national award. The rest of the time he would squat in the dirt at the front of his house picking up pebbles and small sticks that he would roll around in his hands. He had very strong knees, which made him an excellent squatter, even in old age.

After this they worked quietly around the fire to finish preparing the dead birds for the next day's meal.

Other Sanginesini sat together talking. In a corner two brothers whose mother had died recently were arguing. One was always talking about her while the other wanted him to stop because it revived his grief every time her name was mentioned. The former believed he had existed because he was in his mother's thoughts, and now that she was dead he had to find another way to exist. Thus mothers gave life to their children and kept them alive by thinking of them.

Nearby, three women who had been to France to work as wet nurses exchanged tales about the men of the house, who had often participated in their offspring's feeding sessions, demanding a share themselves and attaching themselves to the breast. Having a wet nurse in the house meant the men could continue to bed their wives, who would not sleep with them if they were breastfeeding because they believed that congress curdled the milk. The breastmilk of young Italian women was considered the best, better than the French and the German. The breastmilk of young Italian women was wholesome and had a sunny disposition. The women were laughing and seemed quite pleased with their experiences.

It was dark outside now. When it is dark, when it is night, you should stay inside. Only robbers and whores go about at night, the saying goes.

The night can also be a lonely time, lonelier than the day. As was usual in those days, even back in the village, in the evening the Sanginesini would sit, talk and keep one another company late into the night, for fear of the loneliness that is the lot of all human beings.

This has already been mentioned, but it is good to repeat it to prevent it ever being forgotten.

Bucchione showed his list of vegetables to Beo, who was astonished.

So the sun came up and went down again.

...

After their midday meal on the sixth day, Beo said, 'We could stay here forever, what do you think? These Compitesi sure know how to eat and drink, eh? They're not sick of having us here either, and with any luck they won't be anytime soon!'

Then Sodo, in an unusually philosophical frame of find, responded with, '*Più boschi giri, più lupi trovi*,' suggesting the world was full of wolves, and the more forests you visited the more wolves you encountered. He was shouted down and told to be quiet. It was his way of saying they might as well go home because every place in the world was the same and every place had its dangers. But clearly no-one wanted to hear about it. Even Sodo regretted it as soon as he said it because he didn't really believe the old mill was just another forest and that it was full of wolves. He was very happy to be there.

Nedo, who was only good at making coffee and serving liqueurs and glasses of wine, and was considered a *mezza mestola* – half a bricklayer's trowel, not renowned for his erudition – said, '*Fortunato chi ha il cappotto caldo!* Fortunate is he who has a warm coat!'

He meant it was important to be warm and comfortable and to count your blessings. Nothing else mattered. This really had nothing to do with whether they should go home or not.

To try to move the discussion along, Beo thought he would try again with, '*Vecchi si diventa se non si muore prima.* We will all grow old if we do not die first.'

It was possible he meant that they should stay where they were because their fate would be the same anyway. They would grow old and die regardless of what they did.

Then 'Nibale butted in with his usual gloomy outlook:

> *Tutto passa e tutto muore*
> *Mamma, casa e primo amore.*

> All things must pass, all things must die
> Mother, home and youth's first love.

This was even more bleak than Beo's contribution, but it was to be expected from 'Nibale.

Clearly no-one was interested in addressing the question of leaving the Enchanted Glade, leaving Ponte alle Corti or saying goodbye to the Compitesi, to the food and to the abundance of birdlife, so they talked about cows for a while, noting that, apart from anything else, cows were useful for their body heat – so much so that children were often washed in the stable in a tub filled with water heated over the fireplace, the stable warmed by the breath and bodies of the animals. And yet cows were not always appreciated. A popular saying was, '*Ignorante come una vacca!* As stupid as a cow!'

Bulletta reminded them that Sirio had been caught fornicating with a heifer before he was blown up by the American bomb that fell from the sky, so it was obvious cows had other uses too. This cast a dark cloud over the group and they all wished he hadn't mentioned it. They agreed that Cosetta, his betrothed, should never be told.

Beo made one last attempt at a wise saying, but again it was not relevant to the question at hand:

The Enchanted Glade and the Babbling Brook

Quando il capello dà al bianchino
Lascia la topa e datti al vino.

When your hair is grey and fine
Abandon the fanny and take up the wine.

This time they told him to shut up and turned to look at Bucchione, who until now had been quiet.

Bucchione, who was sucking his cigar and not listening, suddenly realised they were waiting for his contribution. He didn't know what to say. In the end he said, *'Il tempo passa per chi lo puole aspettare.* Time passes for those who can wait.' Meaning, just be still and just be quiet and we'll see what happens. Whether they understood it or not will never be known. Nevertheless, this pronouncement calmed them down and settled the discussion, which was about nothing much and was entering uncharted waters when Bucchione put an end to it.

...

There was a drawn-out musical squawk from God the Father's accordion. This was followed by the plucking of a mandolin string, in turn accompanied by strumming, at which the accordion returned, and pretty soon they were in Arizona, and a few of them were singing snatches of a song about American dreams, illusions and yearning – for a better life, for riches, for dark-skinned Hispanic women and the gentle, sweet happiness that awaited those who emigrated from San Ginese to the Americas.

Zena, whose head and nose were twice as big as his brother Bulletta's, played a virtuoso mandolin. There were also two piano accordionists in the camp: Giorgione the Ancient, who looked much

143

older than his years, and God the Father, who was called that because he had such a high opinion of himself. With a virtuoso mandolin and two accordions, they made enough noise to wake the German dead in Berlin.

So on the evening of the sixth day, Bucchione spoke to Zena (this was in the days before their legendary falling out, after which the two brightest men in the village, the greatest of friends, did not speak to each other for forty years). Zena conferred with Giorgionc and God the Father. The three musicians set up three chairs on an old table. From this rickety podium they could see the dancers, and over the dancers' heads to the wall on the other side. They asked Cosetta to sing. She was a small thing, which is precisely the meaning of her name, but her big chest hid a magnificent voice, mellow and filled with longing, and as dramatic as her flashing brown eyes. Meanwhile Bucchione sent Morena and Paolo running round to tell everyone there would be a dance after the evening meal. The Compitesi were invited too, so it was quite a large party.

After the sun had gone down, Cosetta, her long black hair unleashed around her shoulders and swirling down to her waist, sang as the trio played.

> *Away in Arizona*
> *Homeland of dreams and grand illusions*
> *A lonely guitar player*
> *Excites a thousand skylarks singing.*

And so they tangoed, stamping and gliding and gliding and stamping. You would hardly have thought they were peasants if you'd seen the way they danced so elegantly. They heard the words of the song and you can imagine what happened next.

The Enchanted Glade and the Babbling Brook

It's midnight when it starts
The round of ample pleasure
And in the darkest place
All seek to find their treasure.

As the music penetrated their organisms, meaning their arms, legs, chests, heads and hearts, and other parts, at midnight the round of ample pleasure started. In the darkness everyone was looking for something. Husbands and wives eyed each other like they had when they were sixteen years old. Beo gently stroked Bruna's left buttock for the thousandth time and was left wide-eyed and open-mouthed when she pushed back onto his hand so that he couldn't get it out from beneath her. She rubbed her thigh against his.

A weary bandit leader
Descends the misty sierra mountain
On his pure ivory charger.
A blazing rose of love unbroken.

By the time Cosetta had finished singing to an enthusiastic crowd of dancers and the musical trio were spicing up the evening with a Viennese waltz, half of the available women, and some unavailable ones, had chosen partners and had discreetly slipped away with them into dark corners, behind the bushes and under the trees.

Norato walked over to Cosetta – she who was almost his brother's widow; who wasn't really a widow because she had never been married to Sirio, only betrothed, but nevertheless was expected to behave like a widow and had in fact done that until now. He stood and looked at her, opening his mouth and shutting it like a fool. She opened her mouth and left it open, resting the tip of her tongue against her top teeth, gently nudging her top lip. Norato's blood was warming up, and after her song hers was boiling. They were both experiencing a distant ache flowing from their hearts to their groins that they felt a need to soothe. This is considered normal in young people, and you only hope they can manage their feelings until they are in a position to start a family and look after their children and each other.

> *Her passion is so strong*
> *Her love is without limit*
> *All while they sing their song*
> *A thousand skylarks singing.*

It was the first time he'd kissed a woman on the mouth. To tell the truth, it was Cosetta who kissed Norato. Flashing-eyed Cosetta, who was an expert kisser, and who had kissed his brother Sirio quite a lot before he was blown to pieces, dragged him out of the mill to the riverbank, took the back of his head between both hands and pulled him onto her, slipped her tongue between his lips, rolled it around his mouth and gave him such a thrill that he felt an explosion in his chest and saw a flash of light. She took his left hand and placed it on her right breast, inside her blouse, and it was almost all over for him there and then.

'Bless your hands,' he gasped as she took hold of his member.

When she guided it down to her and let him put it in, the place was warm and inviting, as it should be, and she held him tight with both her hands behind his back and just gave him enough room to wriggle in and out a little. By the time he had gone in all the way the second time he had decided to marry her so that he could do this with her every night for the rest of his life. Norato's member was painfully erect for two hours that night and Cosetta was severely chafed and sore, but despite this, or maybe because of it, they conceived their first daughter, Manola. Unless she had already been conceived when Sirio was still alive. In any case, the Spanish name Manola was in honour of the Hispanic atmosphere generated by the song about Arizona. He would marry her, he said, as soon as they had all finished mourning his brother. *And before it became too obvious that Manola was on the way*, thought Cosetta.

It was the sixth day, after all, when God had told humanity to be fruitful and multiply.

God the Father called Cosetta back for another few songs and the night grew older, noisier and happier, with all the Sanginesini frolicking about in dark corners, dancing and drinking Compitese wine.

Bucchione arrived at a decision about the vegetables.

So the sun came up and went down again.

...

So the sun came up.

It was the morning of the seventh day and they were recovering from the festivities of the night before, lying in small family clusters inside the dark, disused mill, rolling around a little in discomfort if they had consumed too much wine, moaning and resting. They had worked hard every day at eating, drinking, playing cards, hunting, cooking, sleeping, storytelling, debating, dancing, fornicating.

Since arriving they had removed debris from the river, repaired the mill roof and cleared wild *agagi* bushes and blackberry vines from the windows. They had gone hunting and brought back many birds and cleaned them for roasting and eating. This was the beginning of a normal life.

Bucchione and a delegation invited the Compitesi into the Enchanted Glade to discuss a permanent migration to Ponte alle Corti in Compito. The Sanginesini proposed occupying hillside fields and empty houses that had been abandoned by Compitesi who had gone to America. They had left the misery of San Ginese in autumn, and winter was coming. If the war were ever to turn back towards them, in Compito they would enjoy the safety of the hills and the succour of the sun rising and setting on each side of their new home. The neighbours were friendly. The Sanginesini would bring youth and strength to a village in decline. The discussion lasted all morning as both groups weighed the advantages and disadvantages, but the hearts of the Sanginesini were turning and their cardiac organs were empty vessels. Faced with the obligation to decide, they did what many of their countrymen had done in the past when choosing whether to go or whether to stay. The meeting closed without a decision being reached and the council of war dispersed. It would not be easy.

During the night the leaves had started falling. This reminded them that it was well and truly autumn, the precursor to winter that harboured the memory of summer.

The faint creaking sound of the cage, anchored to the chain on the nearby belltower, drifted into their giant shelter.

When they had arrived at the abandoned mill in Compito, they were relieved to be away from the war. In their hearts they yearned for peace, so quickly started to forget the fear and anxiety of their other lives. But now they were finished, and it is a good thing that the Italian word *finiti* can mean exhausted, worn out, spent and done, because they were also all of these things.

The knowledge that had always been there, just below the anxiety in their anxious hearts, started to surface as soon as the cascade of leaves started. The mill house was empty now, but after the war, when people had money to pay for flour and olive oil again, it would be restored. If the people of Compito wanted their mill back, the homeless Sanginesini would have to move out of the Enchanted Glade and into the village.

They needed Bucchione to say something.

Bucchione wondered what would become of them all, although there was really no point wondering – there never is, because it will happen anyway. Within ten years his daughter, Morena, who would remember the Enchanted Glade, would be married. Within eleven years she would give birth to her first son. Within twelve years her husband, Ugo, who would remember the Enchanted Glade, would leave for Australia. But of course, Bucchione didn't know any of this as he addressed the *sfollati*, the displaced.

They just needed Bucchione to say something, and he did, although he could feel the satin wing of the Angel of Sadness brush against his leg.

Bucchione's story wasn't in verse, like the stories told in the village square at nearby Colle by the travelling carnival troupe's hunchback, but he did decide to tell it in the first-person plural. Zena strummed and picked at his mandolin, accompanying his friend for the last time before their grand disagreement.

Bucchione didn't clear his throat or call for their attention. They were already looking at him.

'People … people. It is a well-known fact that the world is a naturally untidy, disordered, chaotic place, where weeds invade fields, and paths become overgrown with tangled blackberry bushes, where tiles shift on roofs, crack and leak, where water seeps in and rots or corrodes everything it touches. We Sanginesini are in the frontline of the war against nature and time, spreading manure, digging and sowing and planting and watering and harvesting, weeding and trimming, cutting and ordering and cleaning and tidying up. Insects and mice, worms and disease attack our crops and animals. Where once there was scrub or arid land, we have brought mown fields and lush crops. The moment we turn one way we are attacked from the other direction. While we rest on a Sunday, the enemy advances. If we are slothful, the enemy charges. As we grow older and our physical and mental strength fades, our children must take over. For this reason we breed. There is no choice. The alternative is to be overwhelmed by the weeds and the pests. The alternative is to drown in shit. And then to die.

'We could of course remain here in Compito, where we have been welcomed, where the soil is fertile and the climate good, where life is sweet. I am ready to sow and plant vegetables right now. I have already prepared a list.' He took his notebook out of his shirt pocket and waved it at them.

The other possibility for them, of course, was to leave San Ginese and go to America (no longer as welcoming as she had been to their fathers, and Australia had not yet opened her doors), but he didn't say that. Nor did he say he had heard rumours that in America and Australia families did not live together and children abandoned their widowed mothers.

Bucchione stopped and looked around, scanning their faces, every single one of them. He said nothing more. They all looked at one another for the first time since the night before they had left the village. Someone coughed.

He waited in silence and they all gasped together at the enormity of what they had done. They had abandoned their cows and pigs and rabbits and chickens, their stables and their fields and their irrigation ditches, Nedo's bar, the communal laundry and bread ovens. The warring armies had gone, but the Sanginesini had not returned to San Ginese, the home of their ancestors, their grandmothers and grandfathers, to the houses where they were born, so old they could crumble at any moment, houses built on the bones of the ancient cemetery, the New Cemetery already overflowing with newer bones, to the stones impregnated with the shit of a thousand summers.

In the shadow of the morning the flames on the candles flickered, and the wicks burned and spluttered gently in their olive oil–filled lids. A strange breeze blew through their skeletons. They were well and truly displaced now. The land, the entire world, had laid a trap for them, had set out to betray them and succeeded, and was even now smothering their fields with weeds, sending maggots and pestilence. The armies of the war, of men and machines, had been replaced by the ancient threats. Who knew what horrors awaited them back in San Ginese were they to return!

As for the fireflies, later that day, after they were gone, well, they just floated and flitted about, jumping from one bush to another, as fireflies do nonchalantly.

They heard the creaking chain.

. . .

They packed their belongings, said goodbye to the Compitesi and stepped into a line behind Bucchione at the natural doorway to the Enchanted Glade and the Babbling Brook, which were bathed in dappled light still, as leaves now began to pour down like soft giant splashes of rain. They stood and waited for the downpour to finish. The falling leaves made a sound like a gentle wind. Soon they were buried up to their knees in brown leaves. Soon they could hear that the rush of falling leaves was easing. And pretty soon it had stopped. And then the silence smothered them. It was over.

And when it was over, it was over. There was nothing more.

Those at the front turned to look at those at the back, and the ones at the back looked at the ones at the front. The Sanginesini took a deep breath.

And then they went home.

The Consequences
of Frostbite

As time passed, whenever the inhabitants of San Ginese talked about a thing, they found themselves saying the thing had been before the war, during the war or after the war. It was the war, the war, the war this and the war that.

It took some time, but in the end they saw that there had been consequences. There were disagreements over what these were. In Nedo's bar long discussions were held that lasted for days, and these became arguments that spilled out onto the courtyard and into the street. One discussion in particular, about the economics of prostitution, became loud and violent and went on into the evening. People stormed out of the bar and back in and threw chairs around and kicked the spittoon. Wives came and tried to drag their husbands home.

It was on one such night that Nello, from Castello, shot past on his bicycle and was catapulted as high as the first floor of Gino's house, where Alfonsina saw him appear briefly at the window.

Nello lived at Castello with his old mother, after his father and brother went to America and never came back. You will remember it was Nello who saw the fireflies when the artillery barrage started.

He was a simple soul with a large oval head that lolled around on his neck, left and right, backwards and forwards, around and around. His mother refused to have him placed in the institution at Marlia. He was committed only after she died.

When he wasn't riding his bike he was walking from Castello, down to Lecci and Centoni, past Pierini, through Villora, and then back up to Castello. On other occasions he would walk to Il Picchio and along the Montanari Hill to the Speranza crossroads, before returning home. If he looked lost, someone would take him by the shoulders and turn him in the right direction and nudge him gently along. Small children sometimes ran after him and pulled faces, and he responded with his own benign grimaces and smirks.

That afternoon he had punctured the front tyre of his bicycle and had strapped a piece of linen around it to stop the air leaking out and just had to remember not to apply the front brakes lest the brake pad catch on the bandage, blocking the wheel, and he be propelled skyward. It turned out that he forgot about this special arrangement and came freewheeling at breakneck speed down the road towards the single corner in the single street of Villora. Someone in the raucous crowd outside Nedo's bar saw what was happening and tried to stop him, but his momentum was too powerful and he slipped through their hands. Approaching the hairpin bend he braked with great force. The bike reared forward and he was thrown off and up, frightening Alfonsina and landing on the awning over her back door, which cushioned his fall and saved his life.

After dusting himself off and complaining of a sore hip and leg and bleeding a little from a blow to his forehead, he was given a glass of rum to calm his emotions and then, head swaying, he limped over to join the group outside the bar and listen to their lively conversation about the consequences of the war. After listening for two hours to various accounts, he announced: 'There were twelve consequences!'

They all looked at him and wondered what he was talking about but quickly dismissed this utterance. Yet if they had reflected for a few moments on what Nello had said, they would have realised that their collective mind had already agreed on many of the consequences, which are presented below. They could not, of course, have known about those that had not yet materialised by the day of Nello's bicycle accident.

...

The first consequence of the war was that for two kilograms of corn meal, you could buy Giorgia.

Before the war, and during it, there was a saying: *Ci sono più puttane a San Ginese che pecore in Maremma* (there are more whores in San Ginese than sheep in Maremma). Maremma is the wild, unspoilt region of Tuscany where sheep and cattle are raised.

Giorgia was one of the whores. Consider this: in the days when

a visit to a brothel cost 5 lire

a packet of cigarettes cost 1 lira

a day's labouring in the fields was paid 5 lire

a night at the opera in Lucca cost 5 lire

1 kilogram of corn meal cost 1.2 lire

you could see Giorgia, who would let you do what you wanted to her in exchange for two kilograms of corn meal, costing 2.4 lire. It would take place either in a neighbouring stable or in a field. The war was here, they said, and no-one had any money so you did what you had to. 'The war was here' – that's how they said it. And Giorgia did what she had to do.

With two kilograms of corn meal, you could feed polenta to a family of seven children, and their parents, twice.

Her husband, Large Joseph, the pig merchant, a gentle-natured soul, was a tall round man with round eyes and a flat nose from whose nostrils long tufts of hair protruded and who wore a battered round brown hat. He never doubted his wife's fidelity, but Large Joseph could not earn enough to support his family by trading in pigs.

Some people said that not all seven of his children were his and that one of his wife's visitors had slipped one in when Large Joseph wasn't looking. When one of the children walked past, the doubters would place two fingers and a thumb under the child's chin and lift its head up and move it around, sideways, a few times, to examine its physiognomy. The alternative gesture was to run your fingers through the child's hair and gently push its head back to perform a facial inspection.

If you ask the people now, no-one can remember what happened to Giorgia – or perhaps they are all lying and prefer to forget what the war made her do and what their fathers did to her.

...

The second consequence of the war was that Il Pallone became busier than Il Bertuccelli.

Il Pallone was not a shoemaker but a cobbler, which means he repaired shoes and did not make them. He had been struck down with poliomyelitis as a child and walked in a strangulated way. Although he was barely able to climb the steep staircase outside the whorehouse just inside the walls in Lucca, he was nevertheless a whoremonger. Having caught syphilis, he produced two damaged children, Titino and Bettina, who were lucky, or unlucky, not to die. Because of the approaching war and the impecuniousness of the local population, who lacked the money to buy new shoes or have shoes made, there was a great demand for the more economical option of his repairs, and he was as busy as he had ever been. He patched shoes and stitched shoes and resoled shoes day and night in his little workshop on the corner next to Gino's house. You could see him working at night through the glass panes of his front door as you were walking past.

At the same time, if you wanted a proper pair of shoes made you would go to Il Bertuccelli, who was a shoemaker. Because of the economic catastrophe that had arrived from America fifteen years before, and because most young men were away from home, having been forced to join the army, he received few orders for shoes. Il Bertuccelli was therefore poor and only made some money after the war was well and truly over, after the Germans had run away and the Americans had gone after them.

Nevertheless, he was a true artist and made exclusive shoes. If he made you a pair, you knew no-one else would have a pair like it. He made the upper of the shoe from one piece of leather, with the only break being the split for the eyelets through which you threaded the laces, under which was the tongue.

His shoes were very expensive but were sought after by young men with a sense of elegance. Ugo bought a black-and-white pair after the Germans had retreated, and his father scolded him soundly for throwing his money away. One more reason to emigrate was to avoid being scolded by your father. However, shoes were important because he was a great dancer, and the women in the crowd watched his feet during tangos and waltzes and fox trots and cha-cha-chas. The women imagined what a man with shoes like that could do to a dancing partner.

...

The third consequence of the war was that many Sanginesini had to disguise their political emotions and at least pretend they supported the authorities in Rome. This was difficult, especially for those villagers who just wanted to work their fields and wander the lanes with their cows, feed the pigs and collect wild plants that they could eat for the evening meal. Bucchione was one of these and did all he could to hide his beliefs and avoid military service.

At first Bucchione and his friend, Il Papa, who was from Pierini, had decided that they would present themselves at the recruitment bureau and leave together. Il Papa was to come round in the morning. However, overnight Bucchione thought about it some more and changed his mind.

When Il Papa arrived and stood at the front of the house calling out to him – 'Hey, Bucchia, let's go!' – Bucchione stuck his head out of his bedroom window and shouted back, 'Papa, I'm not coming. I'm feeling sick.'

Il Papa left for the Russian front by himself and years later, after serving on the Russian front, managed to make it back alive with all his fingers and toes intact.

This was at the start of the war, and Bucchione made up his mind he would stay in the village to look after his family. 'And I am not going to allow myself to be called up and then have to run away to be shot as a deserter either!' he would say to those who cared to listen.

He took to his bed, refused to eat, drank litres of wine and grappa and pots of strong coffee, kept himself awake and didn't shave for a week, all the while smoking the strongest cigars he could find, one after the other, day and night. When the military recruitment office in Pisa wrote to him, he wrote back and told them he was too sick for military service. Then two military police officers turned up with a doctor to examine him. By then he was raving mad, bleary-eyed and gaunt, with large brown patches on his skin where the caffeine and the nicotine had seeped through his veins. Not only was his blood pressure high, but he had developed an irregular heartbeat and started having hallucinations. He hid under the bed and they had to drag him out so the doctor could examine him. His sister Gemma hovered around him all this time, keeping an eye on him, making sure he didn't hurt himself.

The authorities discharged him provisionally, and later, when he found work as a security guard at the Piaggio factory in Pontedera, which built fighter aircraft, discharged him indefinitely. It was work of national significance for the Italian war effort and was counted as military service. Riding his 80 cc Gilera motorcycle across the Lucca plain, through the early evening winter fog, to the plant where one day they would build the Vespa after the war had ended, Bucchione thought about the obstacles that kept getting in the way of his wish for a quiet existence.

On the other hand Il Pechini, from Castello, whose wife was Ugo's schoolteacher, did not have to pretend to be a supporter of the government. His support was genuine. Because he was a devout fascist, but too old to go to the war, they appointed him secretary of the local *fascio*, the party chapter, together with another man from Centoni whose name no-one can remember. The two organised rallies in village squares to encourage the population to donate money and to maintain their fervour in support of the regime. They even held parades, with the village band leading the way, followed by the little children in their *balilla* children's brigade uniforms, the men in their black shirts and the women dressed as traditional rural housewives, all striding through the hamlets of San Ginese. This took them three hours, and the approaching line of marchers, with its distorted fanfares of trumpets, could be heard a kilometre away and annoyed all the secret communist Sanginesini, especially the whole of Villora, which had for generations been the poorest hamlet and was waiting for the real revolution to arrive.

The administration of the *fascio* took place in the *casa del fascio*, a small building next to the church that had been built for the purpose. It was a smooth, white rectangular block with a balcony running the length of the first floor, and the effect was of a kind of modern colonnade with arches. Bucchione said it was called a *casa* because that was the word for house, and when you saw it or went inside you were supposed to feel like it was your home. It was a kind of trick by the government in Rome. On the ground floor was the *dopolavoro*, an after-work club to encourage fellowship among the men of the village, a place where they could drink coffee with cognac and play cards and be in company away from their wives. They did not drink wine there, because to pay money for wine rather than drink the wine you made yourself was a sign that you were *morto di fame*, literally starving to death, meaning you were an incompetent human being, unable to look after your most basic needs, perhaps not even a *cristiano* (which is a rich, poetic Italian word for a human being).

The *dopolavoro*, like the draining of the swamp, was one of Mussolini's ideas. The men were happy to drink and play cards there, but not many believed what they were told to believe. Nedo or his father, who was also called Nedo, like his father before him, opened a *dopolavoro* in Villora too because the one at Castello was too far to walk to after a day's work in the fields. It remained in operation for seventy years.

After the war Il Pechini and his forgotten associate were beaten soundly – *pestati*, crushed – and then bashed again, by the local people who had hated them for years and years but had been afraid to say what they really believed. The two men had been self-important and walked erect and with their chests so puffed out that the tails of their shirts slipped out of their trousers. About men like that they said: '*Aveva la camicia che non gli toccava il culo.* His shirttails did not touch his arse.'

The government was teaching schoolchildren the approved fascist way of standing and walking, and these two men had studied the relevant section of the elementary education programme and applied what they had learned.

At the start they thought they would win. *Vinceremo!* they would shout at the rallies.

...

The fourth consequence of the war was that the old men always remembered the fascist songs. The old men were children then, of course, and the marching music, the fanfares of trumpets and the words filled the hearts of the little boys in their little black shirts and little neckerchiefs, which made them look like boy scouts. Having been taught the words at an age when learning by repetition is very effective, they never forgot them.

Even after they had hidden or washed from their hearts their childish involvement in the *balilla*, old Sanginesini remembered the songs of the regime and the names of the African colonies: Abyssinia (later called Ethiopia), Eritrea, Somalia and Libya. The most popular singers of the time recorded these songs as if they were recording arias by Puccini or Verdi. The dramatic sounds of the orchestras brought to life the pictures in the hearts of the old Sanginesini.

'Faccetta Nera' was a song addressed to a pretty young Abyssinian woman, 'small black face'. The little boys and girls learnt the words that told a story of Italian ships approaching the Abyssinian shore, bringing new laws and a new king. It is a song about doing your duty, black shirts, fallen heroes and liberation. The young woman with the small black face, according to the song, would in due course be shipped to Rome, where she too would wear a black shirt and march before *il Duce* and the king.

'La Sagra di Giarabub' was set at the oasis of Giarabub in Libya. When you listen to the words you are reminded of an old-fashioned theatre stage, with a painted moon nailed to a backdrop that depicts a palm grove, an ancient minaret straddling the dunes, fanfares, flags, explosions and blood. Then you realise the narrator of the story is a dead soldier who refuses his colonel's offer of bread and water, asking instead to be given fire, fire the destroyer, and lead bullets for his musket, swearing that the battle of Giarabub will be the beginning of the end for that bitter foe, the English. The Sanginesini hated the English with a hatred never before experienced. One reason, apart from many other legitimate grievances, was that after the Italian invasion of Ethiopia the English banned imports of wheat and other goods from Italy, and many Sanginesini were impoverished as a result.

Even the children would chant the defiant rhyme of the period:

> *Con un pezzo di pan*
> *e un cipollòn*
> *mando in culo l'Inghilterra*
> *e le sanziòn.*

> All I need is an onion
> to eat and a crust
> and the English sanctions
> can go get fucked.

At Buffalo River in north-east Victoria, Ugo's son would put the blue-labelled Decca record on the old turntable and lower the needle, and Ugo would sing under his breath the words he learnt as an eight-year-old *balilla*, daring the enemy to attack and fight. What he didn't know was that the English force at Giarabub was made up mainly of Australians.

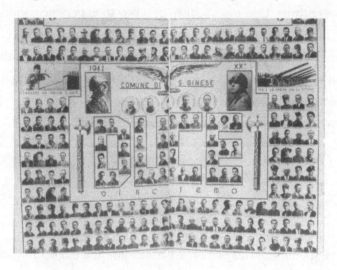

...

The fifth consequence of the war was that Vitale's family of seven first became smaller, and then grew by one.

Before the war, in Vitale's house lived his old parents, Tista and Ancilla, his wife, Irma, daughter, Lida, and sons, Sucker and Ugo. In the middle of the war Tista died, and Ancilla died a year later, and both moved to the final abode of all of us.

Seven became five.

Lida married Leonildo and moved to her husband's house fifty metres away.

Five became four.

Sucker enlisted with the *carabinieri* and moved to the training barracks in Rome. The *carabinieri* was a military force – if you joined them, you could avoid fighting in the proper war, so any sensible person did that. Irma sent parcels of food to Sucker in the post.

Four became three.

So before the war there were seven people in Vitale's house and then there were three. Ugo was shocked as a boy to experience, suddenly, a quiet house. He realised that your life could change unexpectedly, that the people who lived with you could go away, and you could not do anything about it. He decided it would be better if he made his own decisions rather than wait for fate to play its hand.

When Irma gave birth to a late-born son, three became four – but first, three almost became two.

...

The sixth consequence of the war was that Ugo almost died.

Having completed his elementary education, he attended a vocational secondary school at Capannori, where he studied agricultural practice. His education was permanently interrupted when he became sick with double pneumonia and began to spit up blood. He was cupped and given leeches before his mother called the doctor. After visiting Ugo in his sickbed, Doctor Venturini diagnosed *fulminating influenza pneumonia* and didn't tell the family to pray for the sick boy overnight, for fear of frightening them. Despite the discovery of sulfonamide a few years earlier, the war had disrupted supply and there was none for Doctor Venturini to administer. He believed Ugo was on his deathbed, in his grandparents' bed on the first floor, but when he returned in the morning the doctor performed an auscultation and cried out: '*È salvo!* He is saved! I believed I would find him dead!'

A radiological examination performed seventy-eight years later discovered that old Ugo had a large hole in each lung, which he attributed to that *fulminating influenza pneumonia*.

...

The seventh consequence of the war was that Gino came home early.

Gino, who had been called to military service a few months before and had managed to keep away from the fighting, strolled into Villora one day wearing his bright new uniform, polished buttons sparkling and every bit of cloth pressed, with creases in their proper places. He carried his helmet under his left armpit.

If it hadn't been for him turning up out of the blue, no-one would have known that the Italian army had surrendered and was now on the side of the Americans, for San Ginese woke up that morning and everything was the same – except for Gino walking down the road, returning before the real war came and everyone had to leave for the safety of the Enchanted Glade and the Babbling Brook. *'Ehi, Gino, bentornato! L'hai fatta la bella vita, eh?* Welcome back, Gino! Been living it up, eh?'

The villagers couldn't wait to see the Americans. Even though the British were part of the invasion force, the people loved the Americans. Almost all of San Ginese loved the Americans: many of their countrymen had emigrated to America, and the Sanginesini had never understood why they should fight the Americans in a war. As American convoys drove through the villages of Italy, trucks and jeeps carrying happy soldiers who gave sweets and chocolate to children, the people shouted: *'Gli americani! Gli americani!'*

...

The eighth consequence of the war was that the young people of the village organised chicken feasts, to which whoever could spare one would bring a roast chicken. They would gather a small orchestra, with

Zena on accordion or mandolin, Giorgione, Pittone and Padreterno on accordion, and Baby (pronounced *bebi*), a name brought back from California, on clarinet. Sometimes there was a guitarist. It was in Vitale's large front room that they all drank and danced and then ate the chickens. Afterwards there were almond cakes that had been baked especially for the occasion.

In the last year of the war, well after the Germans had run away and settled down along a defensive front in the Garfagnana hills, American soldiers on leave from the base at Livorno, on the coast, would come to the chicken feasts to enjoy the company and the other benefits of the young women, who pleaded to be kidnapped and taken to America. When they got to know them, the young women found the Americans were not always happy, friendly and generous. For these later chicken feasts, a fee would be charged.

. . .

The ninth consequence of the war was that everyone became afraid of everything, whether it was when the Americans were bombing Livorno and their squadrons flew over the village, or after the armistice, when the Germans were the enemy and the Luftwaffe took its turn. They became afraid and hid.

The men who had avoided military service or who had come home when the Italian forces collapsed, men like Gino and Danny, hid from the Germans in the long grass, with the cows. They were reluctant to go out onto the roads and into their fields with their carts and working animals. They had heard stories that in nearby towns the German war planes fired machine-guns at slow-moving carts laden with hay, while small patrols wandering about the countryside used flamethrowers to set fire to clumps of reeds and tangled *agagi* bushes where men might be hiding. The Sanginesini heard rumours they also burned carts with the cows still attached. The sound of the aeroplanes overhead made you run to the cesspit.

At night a few people gathered around the radio in Nedo's bar to hear reports on the progress of the war, and they feared the worst. Meanwhile, the word spread quickly if a brother or father away at the war had stopped writing, or his letters were no longer arriving, or he had disappeared into the fog on a distant battlefield. Everyone feared the sudden absence of news.

Enzo, who was Vitale's nephew, and Ugo rode their bicycles to the station in Lucca, where Enzo caught the train to Bolzano, near the Austrian border, to report for duty at the barracks there. Ugo brought his riderless bike back to the village. On the day Enzo arrived in Bolzano, the armistice had just been signed and the Germans were now the enemy, so they took him as he got off the train and he was sent to a labour camp, where he later died. A lieutenant-ranked chaplain at the labour camp wrote to give Enzo's mother the news. Her fear was replaced by the kind of grief that filled every room in her house. After the war the same chaplain, who had made Enzo a solemn promise before he died, delivered his personal effects to his mother. Enzo had never worn his uniform.

Because of the fear, villagers made plans. In Vitale's vegetable garden below the ancient fig tree was a large hole in the ground where men hid, if there was time to hide, when a German patrol was going through the village looking for slave labour to send to the fatherland.

In the vegetable garden Vitale had also buried a large jar full of money, which would be useful if members of the family were taken or separated.

'Those of us who survive can come back here and get the money,' he told his children. 'If something happens and we can get away, your mother and I will walk to Compito through Padule and then turn right to reach Centoni before continuing on our way into the hills. We should all walk separately so that if we are ambushed, not all of us will die.'

Fear meant you lied to save your life so you could help your family. In the year Ugo came of age, at the medical examination for his military service, which required a battery of tests, he was fortunately diagnosed with a heart murmur by the doctor who was Vitale's friend. The military doctor classified him as unfit for military service. In his long life Ugo only mentioned this cardiac defect once or twice, as he was embarrassed by the lie the doctor had told and at his father's complicity in it, although generally speaking there was no dishonour in wishing to avoid being killed in a war.

Fear meant that Danny, who was Gino's and Ugo's cousin, hid in the cave underneath Lilì's house. When he was discovered by two German soldiers, they dragged him out and into the courtyard by the scruff of the neck and at the point of their guns. In desperation, Danny escaped. His plan was a simple one: to break free and run. And run. Between houses and stables and through woodsheds, down stone steps jutting out from retaining walls. They immediately opened fire with their Maschinengewehr 42 automatic weapons and missed.

Danny fled to the hole in the side of the terraced hillside behind Lida's house. Gino was already there, perfectly hidden in the cavity dug into the embankment, behind long grass and bushes, and he reproached Danny for possibly leading the Germans to him. Gino was afraid that the Germans would use flamethrowers to flush them out. But no-one came.

Morena, who was eight years old, never forgot how the sound of flying bombs made her intestines gurgle so that she ran to the chamber-pot every time. Her friend Erica, well into the next century – when

Erica had become the second-oldest person in the village, when all the migrants had sailed away and a few had returned, and most had become lost around the world and their children and grandchildren had barely even heard of San Ginese – Erica, standing in front of her green-washed house on a sunny spring day, as she waited for an Albanian to come to weed her small garden, would look you in the face and say, '*Ohimè! Che paura!* How afraid we all were!' *Ohimè!* is the word that you use when you wish to convey physical or spiritual dejection, dismay or pain.

More than seventy years later, what Erica remembered most of all was the fear. The great fear experienced by the people is a fact that many who are not directly affected forget when talking about a war.

...

The tenth consequence of the war was that it displaced entire populations of innocents.

Individuals and small groups wandered in, stumbled in, to San Ginese from the large towns and cities as the armies bombed each other. Stables, wine cellars and huts were slowly occupied by frightened, hungry people, until they overflowed. What else could the villagers do but shelter and feed them? Many of the displaced fleeing the war were from Livorno, which is also the place where the large white homonymous chicken, the livornese, comes from. Just like the chickens, people from Livorno are called livornesi.

Vitale sheltered in his stable in the Mattei Courtyard, a fugitive from the fighting in Livorno. One morning a German soldier came, pushing a wheelbarrow in which he was carrying his standard-issue rifle. In the middle of the courtyard were two sacks of wheat that had been threshed the night before. He ordered the guest to lift both sacks into his wheelbarrow. The man obeyed, but as the German was leaving with his heavy load, straining up the slight incline and back onto the street, the Livornese suggested with enthusiasm to Vitale that they kill him.

Vitale rejected this proposal, saying, 'No. It is possible that he is one of those innocent Germans and that he just wants to eat.'

...

The eleventh consequence of the war was that the work of the peasant was never the same.

The sacks of grain in Vitale's courtyard taken by the German were a sign of the slowing of agricultural work in the years of the war. The communal mechanical thresher had not visited San Ginese for a long time, so the work had to be done as it was in the olden days. Bundles of wheat were spread out in the courtyards and beaten with the *correggiato*, a flail made of two large sticks attached to each other at the extremities with a small chain or piece of leather. You held one of the sticks in one or both hands and swung the implement over your shoulder, then brought it down with force to strike the pile of wheat, each blow separating the chaff from the grain.

The mechanical thresher later returned and then was used almost all the time by everyone, even those who before the war had grumbled about modern contraptions. In addition, instead of cutting wheat and grass by hand with a long-handled scythe, called a *frullana* (from the original *friulana*), you now attached a *moa* to the cow (*moa* being a distortion of the English word *mower*, another word brought back from California) and did the harvesting that way.

After the war, villagers also acquired water pumps, most of which were manufactured in Mantua by the Officina Colorni engineering workshop. Bucchione bought a pump from the American army, which was disposing of equipment it no longer needed.

Of course, pumps were also used to irrigate crops at the appropriate time. Once, they had used donkeys to drive irrigation wheels. Now these new pumps were so effective and saved so much work and made so much money that they were like donkeys shitting Napoleon gold coins. Bucchione called his pump just that: '*un miccio che caca marenghi.*'

...

The twelfth consequence of the war was not felt for many years, so did not form part of the discussion in front of Nedo's bar on the day of Nello's accident.

If you tried to argue that the twelfth was not a true consequence of the war but that it was simply a matter of a correlation without causation, it would be up to you to provide an alternative explanation for the events that followed. In any case, who is to say why some things happen and some things don't?

The twelfth consequence consisted of two parts, having one Primary Cause.

The first part concerned Remo Sportelli, who did not have a wife. He lived with a woman who, people said, did the housework and looked after him. This was the same thing people would say about the parish priest, that he had a housekeeper who did the housework and looked after him. It was normal for a man to be looked after. A man needed looking after, and usually a wife did that. A man who for one reason or the other, and usually it was the other, did not have a wife made alternative arrangements. About Remo Sportelli they would say, 'He has a woman who does the housework and looks after him,' and their left nostril, or their right nostril, would twitch, producing what looked like a wink of their left eye, or their right (the side was optional), as if to say *well, you know what is going on there.*

Remo was almost married once, but in the end the woman could not countenance the touch of his three-fingered left hand on her breast or the brush of his two-toed right foot against her leg in the marital bed she imagined. Her mother scolded her, praising Remo's character and military service and reminding her of a long, easy passage through life lubricated by government pay for easy work and a government pension, but the mother's efforts were in vain.

When Remo Sportelli the soldier returned from the Russian front, after the Russian snow had bitten off two of the fingers on his left hand and three of the toes on his right foot, the authorities had given him preferential employment as the teacher of artistic education at the junior secondary school in San Leonardo.

He taught the children to draw what was in front of their eyes, not what they saw in their fantasy. This was the fundamental principle of artistic education. The children always began by drawing trees with a round green ball, which was the crown, resting on a brown pedestal, which was the trunk. Remo knew that people, in this case the schoolchildren, saw what they wanted to see, not what was there.

From the age of twenty-two years Remo's teacher's pay, and the special war emolument issued as compensation for the loss of the digits of his hand and foot, ensured a good enough income that, by the time Ugo returned to Italy the first time, Remo was almost wealthy. His income was much greater than the usual pay for a person of his origins and he was able to save much of it to buy land. He had no wife and no children to support, just a frugal housekeeper.

With the fruit of his absent digits Remo bought land on a hillside, behind which grew a large pine forest, in a place called Palaiola, on the periphery of San Ginese. He built a magnificent stone house at the front of the forest and sold the land below his house on the left to Ugo, who wanted to build a house with Australian money, like Sucker had done.

Remo Sportelli also sold land below his property on the right to Il Bacchi, who would build a house for his daughter. Il Bacchi's daughter's house would be a grand house on a hillside in Tuscany, with a beautiful view.

Il Bacchi's daughter and son-in-law had emigrated to England, and the old man's grandchildren, two girls and a boy, were born there. Il Bacchi and his wife were very lonely, although the daughter brought her family to visit her elderly parents twice a year, staying with them each time for two weeks in San Ginese, where she was born. Everyone knows the loneliness of the old is an aching, desolate bleakness. With age all hope leaks out from the soul and physical ailments bedevil the body. The illumination and warmth of the sunshine that children bring to the lives of old people is immeasurable. It soothes the bones and the muscles and the ligaments and restores the soul.

When the daughter decided to return to Italy permanently, her father was overjoyed. She asked him to build her a house and he started immediately, doing all the work himself, although he was no longer young, only calling in workers when it became too much for him. He worked every day for two years. The neighbours watched him laying bricks, pouring concrete and struggling to push his wheelbarrow through the mud in winter.

He was still building it when Ugo left to return to Australia, and many years later Ugo heard that he had died, but this was only after his daughter had changed her mind and decided to remain in England forever with her husband and the old man's grandchildren. Forever.

As a teacher of artistic education, Remo knew that Il Bacchi saw what he wanted to see in his daughter's request. Il Bacchi saw family closeness and unity and happiness. When he sold the land Remo knew that the daughter might break her father's heart, but there was no obligation on Remo to warn the old man.

And so it was that because of the war, because of frostbite on the Russian front (the Primary Cause), Remo Sportelli, who did not have a wife and was unencumbered and could live frugally, was able to save his veteran's pay and impairment pension supplement to buy land and sell it to Il Bacchi, who built a house for a daughter who broke his heart.

. . .

The second part of the twelfth consequence was that Ugo built a house on Remo Sportelli's land too, using Australian money, just as Sucker did in Monkey's Field.

When Ugo bought the land, Remo knew what Ugo saw in that land. Ugo saw happiness for himself and his family. Ugo also saw Laurence Olivier as Heathcliff returning to the place that had been a misery when he was a young man. Having made his fortune he would show everyone in San Ginese how well he had done, that he could buy land and build a grand house with a forest behind it on a hillside in Tuscany.

Remo knew, just as he knew the impulses of the children in the classroom, that Ugo was seeing what he wanted to see, not the tree as it truly was in the field.

And so it was that because of the war, because of frostbite on the Russian front (the Primary Cause), Remo Sportelli, who did not have a wife and was unencumbered and could live frugally, sold the land to Ugo, and Ugo built the house, and then Ugo and his wife Morena were unhappy and returned to Australia, and as a result of all this Morena ran away, which is what women did in those days, because they were prisoners and they were always trying to escape, like birds in a cage, like a *tordo* (which is a thrush) or a *fringuello* (which is a chaffinch).

You could say that such were the consequences of frostbite, but it would be absurd if you did because the matter was more complicated than that.

THE VISITOR

A Modest Tour
of San Ginese

If a man who was born in San Ginese were to return after being away in Australia for many years, he would be like a visitor from abroad, a tourist.

People would think it was unusual for a grown man to walk along the road for the purpose of recreation on a sunny morning, wearing a hat for shade, or on an overcast afternoon, in the rain, carrying an umbrella. They would think it was very unusual if he walked that route three times in one day with only minor deviations, walking for two hours each time. They would not know that inside the Visitor there burned a strong desire to know the name of every person in the three cemeteries, where he would spend much of his time. They would not know that inside the Visitor there burned a strong desire to know everything there was to know about San Ginese and that this desire extended to knowing the names of the plants that grew there.

As he walked he might study the plants growing along the verge, take photographs and ask his cousin for their names later, writing everything down in a small black notebook. If they knew that he was doing this too, they would think he was in actuality mad, a mad foreigner, of which there have been many in Tuscany since the English started their Grand Tours of Europe in the seventeenth century.

These are the plants he would discover:

graminacea	graminaceous plants, grass
tarasacco (*piscialetto*)	dandelion (*piss-a-bed*), a diuretic plant
vitalba	an edible climbing plant, good for use in a frittata
cardo selvatico spinoso	wild thistle, an ancient plant present in Greek and Germanic myth
gigaro	arum; toxic
papaveri	poppies; the subject of a popular song, 'Papaveri e papere'
edera	hedera, common ivy; the subject of another popular song, 'L'Edera'
rogna	untranslatable dialect; has a yellow flower
trifoglio	clover, trefoil (genus *Trifolium*); literally 'three leaves'
fiore di trifoglio	clover flower
agagio	a species of acacia that has invaded the abandoned hillsides and fields
menta selvatica	wild mint; perennial
cipressi	pencil pine cypress; often featured in tourist brochures
sambuco	elder, whose white flower is of no use at all, for anything, according to some Sanginesini, while others cook them in fritters; generally toxic
rovo	blackberry, combining with the agagio to make hillsides and terraces impenetrable
gelso	mulberry; has an edible fruit; used in silkworm breeding, as an ornamental plant and for firewood
pioppo	poplar; popular for firewood. Tuscans are fond of this tree.

The Visitor

The Visitor would recommend that for best results the English reader pronounce aloud the Italian words in the table.

The Visitor would notice how the *agagio* was invading the abandoned vineyard terraces and olive groves and the hillsides. He would come to understand that the *agagio* is a great infester of land. It is a tree and a weed at the same time. It is ambitious and aggressive – not merely assertive but aggressive. It was useful as long as there were peasants working the land and it was kept under control. It is a hard wood, ideal for making wheels for carts, spokes for the wheels and posts for supporting grapevines.

'*Ne tagli uno ne spuntano dieci*,' they say. 'Cut one and ten will grow.'

His cousin would tell him that as firewood it is despised because it does not burn well, yet it is popular because it is cheap. His cousin would also tell him that the flower of the *agagio* is sweet and edible and is often added to a *frittata*. He would ascertain directly that the *agagio* will quickly form isolated copses that reach out to one another and form entanglements until they become complicated, snarled forests inside which razor-sharp blackberry vines proliferate.

The Visitor would walk on, past the church with the ancient belltower where he was baptised. Here the bones of his ancestor Genesius lie in an ossuary under a monument to the fallen of the Great War, in a courtyard from which you can see the smoking, steaming chimney stacks of the Porcari pulp mills and the paper and cardboard factories. He would continue past the old house on the right, on the edge of the road, below which the hillside drops away steeply. The house grips the earth on the side of the hill, holding on for dear life. This is the school that Ugo attended as a little boy.

On the high side of the hill on the left is a large agricultural estate Ugo almost purchased on his first failed attempt to abandon Australia and return home.

From the hill near the church the Visitor would see the hamlet of Pierini, in a narrow valley that, if San Ginese were a lizard, would be between the flank and the resting rear right leg of the lizard.

...

After the botanical walk the Visitor might decide to walk between the agglomeration of small hamlets that make up the village of San Ginese. If he did, he would walk through the centre of Villora, past Tista's house, where he, the Visitor, was born, and where Ugo was born; past the house opposite, where Tommaso the Killer lived and was arrested by the running police in their spectacular uniforms; past the house where the imbeciles lived; past the place on the corner where the Albanians live now; past the house of Julio the Orphan, who cared for the animals when the villagers fled to Compito during the German retreat; down past Lida's house; and to the house of Sucker in Monkey's Field (which Vitale bought with money he brought back from America), where the widowed Adulteress lives. Then he would follow the road on the right below the hill as far as Centoni (the same road the villagers took when they marched out to seek refuge in the Enchanted Glade). Just before entering Centoni, inside the cutting with raised terraces on each side, he would meet a migrant from Naples, a woman planting onions, whom he had never seen before because he had been away for so long and she had arrived after he had left. He would stop to talk to her and tell her that, like her, he was from outside (that's what they say there, literally, 'outside'), having come from Australia.

He would not tell her that he had been back twice before, for one year and then two years, to attend the high school in San Leonardo and later the university in Pisa. On both these occasions his mother and father would decide to return permanently to San Ginese and bring him with them. Their two attempts at resettlement would fail. Then, after staying away for twenty years, he would begin a series of short visits, each a few years apart, of which this was one.

After leaving Centoni (where Derì lived), the Visitor would climb the steep *servette* section of road with two sharp bends and, at Lecci, instead of turning left, towards the refuge in the hills, he would turn right, towards Castello.

But before we follow the Visitor to Castello, let him take us back two kilometres or so ...

The Adulteress

The Adulteress sits at the front window on the right of the house as the Visitor approaches, walking down the slope from Villora. She waves to him briefly when she recognises him, and gives a little square smile. It's a short wave, as if she has waved at him and has lost interest and is now searching for someone else to wave at as she sits at the window, pedalling her little machine to keep the blood circulating through her ancient legs. This is the woman people say has not yet died because she has forgotten to.

The Adulteress sits at the front window of the house her husband, Sucker, built with the money he made in Australia. Sucker and his brother Ugo worked long and difficult hours at Buffalo River. One year, after a monstrous hailstorm shredded the leaves, they laboured ankle-deep in mud and plant debris to bring in every scrap of prime tobacco leaf. The soil was good, rich and friable on the river flat, and the tobacco grew well, and Ugo made a lot of money in those paddocks over many years. His brother joined him for three of those rich harvests.

...

The Adulteress sits at the front window and remembers Sucker, her unfaithful husband, who at the start courted her the way he courted anything with two legs and a skirt (or so they said). One day she announced she was pregnant. By the time it was clear she was not, they were married.

The newlyweds rented a house. One day Sucker saw his wife walking out of a neighbour's stable and was suspicious. He set about spying on her to see if he could catch her in the act. The night it happened he was in a neighbouring town, Viareggio, visiting the wife of another man. He left Ugo on watch.

On the night in question Ugo saw Beppino, the milkman from neighbouring Picchio, whose inhabitants were notorious good-for-nothings, enter through the front door of the house. Beppino came out two hours later adjusting his belt, of course, and his hat. He entered through the front door and came out the back.

Sucker prevailed on the men of the village to sign statements as evidence of his wife's adultery. His own absence on the night of the crime was explained by the need to discuss the purchase of a cow, to which the vendor usefully testified. The sale, of course, did not go ahead and there was never a word uttered about Sucker's own infidelity on the same night.

When questioned, the Adulteress admitted only that she and Beppino had met and talked about the milk collection and delivery. She was grateful for Beppino's company, as her husband was away. Her husband's mother and father and her sister-in-law were visiting neighbours that night and were not free to keep her company, and, besides, the strength of their relationship was not such that she could impose on them her presence – the presence of a lonely, abandoned wife, whose husband was a philanderer.

When she raised with the investigating magistrate an accusation against her husband, it was quickly dismissed by the man in black for lack of evidence. She had no witnesses, whereas her husband had half the village supporting his account of events.

The law she had broken, which was enacted by the fascist government in 1930, clearly spelled out that a single instance of adultery by a woman constituted a violation of the legislator's decree. For a man, a husband, a breach would have to be repeated, and would need to culminate in the abandonment of the family before he could be charged and possibly punished. Nothing of the sort could be proven against Sucker, although he was indeed guilty of adultery, and his poor wife did not even try.

...

The Adulteress sits at the front window on the right of the house as the Visitor walks down the slope from Villora. She waves to him briefly when she recognises him.

She was convicted of adultery and her punishment was left to her husband to decide, subject to a prohibition against physical punishment. The normal consequence of her conduct was banishment from the village, and banished she was, to a small abandoned house at Castello, near the hamlet of Collina, which was her birthplace, while their boy, Vito, lived with his grandparents. She took in piecework, knitting jumpers and scarves, and with her mother's help was able to feed herself for a year, although her life was a misery.

Sucker, meanwhile, pursued with renewed vigour his previous pursuits, involving multiple women. He was invigorated now and imbued with a strong sense of justification – the same sense that ensured that for the rest of his life he would bed one woman after another and ignore his wife entirely, without any compunction or guilt. He always reminded her that she was lucky he had taken her back, which by the way he did, most of all for the sake of Vito, who was eight years old at the time his mother met Beppino in the dark house in the row of houses in front of the *Aia dei Mattei*, the Mattei Courtyard, while Sucker visited his woman in Viareggio, on the Tuscan Riviera.

Sucker took his adulterous wife back because no-one knew what else you could do with a wife like that, especially as there was a child to raise. He took her back and, in her, had himself a servant to raise Vito – who remained unusually short, having inherited the blood of the short men like Vitale and Tista, not that of the tall men from Colognora, on Irma's side of the family – and a housekeeper to cook and clean with no expectation that he, Sucker, ought to contribute anything other than a roof over their heads and food on their table.

And so the family lived in the house Sucker built with the money he brought back from Australia, built in a field bought with the money his father made in America.

The Visitor would reflect on this – the field, the house, Australian money, American money – as he approaches.

After his return from Australia and for the rest of his life, Sucker worked as a skilled bricklayer and mason on building sites with his cousin Gino. He was a good provider. He doted on his son and later his grandchildren. He never bedded his Adulteress again, and she was celibate for the next sixty years and more. He treated her badly, with disdain, showing her no respect, but she always spoke well of him, as if there were a great love between them.

...

Sucker died at a relatively young age many years ago, his Clark Gable hair grey but still thick, his teeth perfect, and he is buried in the New Cemetery of San Ginese with his failed liver. At first people said it was cirrhosis caused by a combination of Malta fever, which he had contracted when he was young, and excessive consumption of wine. In the end it was determined he had caught an infectious liver disease from the instruments of a dentist who practised poor hygiene in his clinic. Sucker was proud of his perfect hair and his perfect teeth. The hair was always full and undulating, gently preserved in a net as he lay his head on his pillow at night. He took great care to maintain both his coiffure and his dentition as he aged, thus preserving his attractiveness to women.

...

So Sucker dies, and by the time his widow comes to be sitting regularly at the window in her husband's house, to the right of the front door, everyone who had been a party to, first, the criminal charge against her, brought ten years after the war ended, and second, her conviction for adultery, is also dead (except, at the time of writing, for Ugo).

She sits there, her feet on the pedals of the leg exerciser, and looks up along the length of the road winding down from the village and sees the Visitor walking towards her. Her accusers are dead: the witnesses who testified, the policeman who arrested her, the investigating magistrate; all those who banished her from the village are dead. The innocent who watched and were silent are dead too, including her mother, who lived to be ninety-three. She pedals, and is also now ninety-three years old. Only Ugo is alive, and he went to Australia, three years after he reported her infidelity to his older brother.

She has outlived Sucker by thirty years. At every opportunity she shows you photographs of her handsome husband. What lovely hair. What perfect teeth.

Beppino emigrated to South Africa with his wife and children.

The 1930 adultery law was repealed in 1969.

The Dinner of the Pig

Giuseppe Dal Porto was born a moody man. When he returned from *la guerra del quindici–diciotto*, the war of fifteen to eighteen, which is what the Italians call it, during which he was a prisoner of the Austrians, under whom he endured enormous suffering due to cold and hunger, he was even moodier. Like all the men of his time he yearned for a male heir, so his wife, Carolina, had to bear him three daughters before Derì was born. The moody Giuseppe made arrangements, while living, to disinherit his daughters with little compensation so that the estate could go entirely to the newly born Derì.

In his final years Giuseppe often visited Villora to stay with his daughter Alfonsina, who had married Gino. They would position him on a kitchen chair on the outer gravel shoulder of the hairpin bend (where he eventually died), in front of the place where the mythical stone was buried in the foundations of Gino's house.

The warmth of the sun gave comfort to his bones, the movement of the air brought inspiration to his skin, and the passing people brought interest to his eyes and ears. There he sat, a dapper old man wearing a brown tweed trilby hat, asleep in the sun, the crook of his walking stick hooked over his knee or, arms extended, both hands resting one on top of the other on the stick, which was planted firmly in front of him in the dirt.

As his ageing, diseased brain deteriorated, the arms and hands retreated to his lap where he held them gently cupped, one inside the other. He had been a medium-sized compact man, always impeccably turned out in a leather jacket, his bearing elegant, in the days when appearances counted. No-one would have guessed he was once the most astute and admired livestock broker in the district. He had been to America twice and had done well and, having laid the foundation, continued to build his fortune from shrewdness in business in San Ginese and the surrounding district.

...

Of course, everyone expected Derì to take over the family business, but the signs were not good from the start.

As the boy grew, the effect of the Great War on Giuseppe produced a kind of silent conflict between father and son. The father's moodiness was converted into secret discontent at the imperfections of the son. The father consoled himself with the thought that it could have been worse, that the son could have been born a hunchback, but this attempt at consolation was to no avail. The son matured in fits and starts. Everyone waited for the young boy to become a man, but the father's hidden disappointment created in the boy a wavering uncertainty. That Giuseppe Dal Porto had enjoyed enormous respect in the district and brought his family material comfort did not make life easy for Derì, who found it impossible to live up to his father's example. And so it happened that as he struggled to rise above his father's moods, Derì was always either in ecstasy about some plan he had just excogitated or else was sinking under the weight of his sins. The coming of the Second World War and the economic decline that accompanied it did not help him, although no-one believed it was the reason for his lack of business success.

When Derì's blonde wife produced, at the first attempt, a male heir, whom they named after the grandfather, well, that was that. Derì came under an immediate paternal injunction to stop producing offspring for fear of diluting the family fortune. He and his blonde wife acquiesced. Giuseppe, the grandson of Giuseppe, remained an only child.

. . .

For a hundred years America had been El Dorado and everybody had gone looking for it, but when America came to neighbouring San Leonardo in the form of the Palazzo Cinematografico, Derì could see no point in sailing across the seas. He went to the cinema instead. Thinking he could become a star didn't make him one, however, and as the years passed the suspicion that he would never be a star started to weigh on him and, when he wasn't being playful, he felt thwarted, became gloomy and drank the cloudy light-red wine of San Ginese.

When Giuseppe's son Derì got drunk, he sang 'Signorinella'. It was one of those popular songs from the time before the factories were built at Porcari, on the other side of the swamp. After the electricity came you could hear the song coming out of people's windows all over San Ginese. They played it on the wireless, and the entire nation sang along to it for thirty years.

The words of the song tell the story of young, thwarted love, remembered many years later when the burden of middle age starts to wear you down. The sentiments expressed belong to another time and place and are not easily understood nowadays. In any case, men no longer think of women that way, and certainly don't address them as the song does.

The song perfectly described the permanent state of Derì's heart, which to him was by far the most important organ, as it could sweep you on waves of passionate melancholy away from San Ginese, out over the Mediterranean, across the Atlantic Ocean, past the Statue of Liberty in New York Harbor, and overland by train to California, a real journey his father had twice undertaken and which he only dreamed about. During these reveries, overcome by emotion, from the corner of his eye he saw himself on a cinema screen, the wrist of his cigarette hand cocked, elbow pressed against hip, a quizzical eyebrow raised, scrutinising with heavy-lidded eyes the red-lipped blonde who was watching him through wisps of curling smoke. The yearning for a long-lost young love became the yearning for his long-lost young life.

These few words give a taste of the mood of the song:

> *E gli anni e i giorni passano*
> *Eguali e grigi, con monotonia*
> *Le nostre foglie più non rinverdiscono*
> *Signorinella, che malinconia!*

Days and years have passed since then
All the same, grey and monotonous
The leaves on the trees will never be green again
Oh sweet young girl, there is such sadness in my life!

It was just the way Derì was, and there was nothing anyone could do about it.

Like Cyrano de Bergerac, Derì had an interesting long nose with a small knob on the tip. It was this that attracted the women, probably for its promise of other possibilities, but so did his thick brown hair – all tight little curls and undulations through which they could run their thick peasant-girl fingers – and his wistful air, wet eyes and misty gaze.

Derì took after his father in one thing at least: he liked to dress well, and whenever he turned up at Villora to visit his married sisters he was freshly bathed and his hair was neatly combed. He swaggered just enough, the metal press studs on his snug brown leather jacket were fastened and there was just the slightest suggestion of a paunch, which women rubbed when their husbands, fathers and brothers weren't looking.

When he was young he was engaged to a girl called Neva, who was from Massa Macinaia. A few years into the betrothal he tired of her but didn't know how to end the relationship. If he heard she was in the vicinity, he would hide in the house, not going out for days to avoid seeing her. In those times women could be ruined if they were the subject of a long engagement that was later broken off. What 'ruined' meant was that their emotional innocence and fresh affection was no longer available for another man to enjoy. Innocence and freshness were prized qualities in a woman. Derì was not a ruiner of women, though. It was the women who sought him out, and you could say they ruined themselves.

In the end Neva's father rode his horse all the way from Massa Macinaia, appeared at the door and demanded to know what Derì's intentions were. It was left to Carolina, Deri's mother, to give the man the bad news while her son hid in his bedroom.

There were two other women, twins, beautiful and in love with him, who lived at the top of the hill, near the church. Their fingers were long and slender, with just the right amount of plumpness around the phalanges and pretty, little, sweet kissable creases on each knuckle. Their pink fingertips were in particular nicely full and rounded, the skin so delicate and translucent you could see the blood coursing through them.

For those days they were also exceptional women, because one was a professor of literature and the other a primary-school teacher. The Italians revere their national literature and worship anyone who has studied it seriously and has become an expert in it, and their primary-school teachers remind them of their mothers as young women and so they adore them too.

One day Derì went to visit the literature professor to offer his condolences on the death of her mother. He expected (and hoped) to find her in deep mourning, and had prepared himself for an encounter with great, uplifting grief, believing the heightened sensitivity necessary to appreciate and teach great works of art would render her particularly vulnerable to deep emotional pain. Instead she started showing him saucy photographs of herself in her swimming costume at Viareggio, posing on the sand this way and that, hand on hip, looking back over her shoulder at the camera, emphasising her flank and her leg, eyelids half-closed. After that he never thought of her again.

As for the primary-school teacher, she pined for him for years and often made excuses so she could walk past his house, hoping to be seen by him. She was known to sleepwalk down the San Ginese hill from Lecci in the moonlight and stand perfectly still and silent in the main street below his bedroom window, even after he was married. Although he never laid a finger on her, she was considered spoiled because her intense love for him had rendered her unfit for marriage to anyone else. How could anyone spend their life with a woman whose heart had been ground to dust?

Derì was a ladies' man in his youth, but after marrying he stopped his womanising, although the women kept coming. The one he ended up with was a wickedly sensuous and frivolous blonde from the Pieve San Paolo whom he lusted after with such urgency that his groin hurt for months before the wedding night.

...

Now, as everyone knows, there are certain events in every life that characterise it.

Late one night, as Derì was walking home to Centoni from Nedo's bar, he arrived at the bottom of the Servette, the steep winding road near Palazzo, when he stumbled onto a brawl between a gang of young men from San Leonardo and some Sanginesini. The fight was over the sister of one of the Sanginesini, whose virginity had been questioned. Women were a common source of strife among the peasantry in those days. The Sanginesini were getting the worst of it when Derì charged in and, in a frenzy of punching, kicking, elbowing, head-butting and scratching, single-handedly turned the tables on the rival mob. As he ran towards the affray, he could see the long shot first, then the medium shot and finally the close-up.

Pittone, a local poet, penned some colourful verses that immortalised the fracas and Derì's role in it. One verse read as follows:

Si sentì un gran urlo
Era Buccello in lite con Piturlo.

We knew from the deafening shout that arose
that Buccello and Piturlo had come to blows.

Buccello and *Piturlo* were nicknames for the young men from San
Ginese and San Leonardo respectively.

But the occasion that engraved his name forever in everyone's
store of memories was the Dinner of the Pig.

...

One December night Derì got drunk. It was during the Dinner of
the Pig, a feast of celebration held after the annual pig had been
slaughtered and minced into pork sausages and salami of various
kinds and hung up to cure, its hams dressed and buried in salt presses,
and various other delicacies stored in barrels. The pig was always
killed in December because there were no flies then and the cold
prevented the meat from spoiling, but the cold also encouraged the
men to drink the cloudy local wine, white or red, or a small glass of
rum for the physical and emotional warmth it brought.

It was Gino's pig, so the Dinner of the Pig was being held in Gino's
house. Gino's wife, Alfonsina, Derì's sister, made a large pot of risotto
from the unused remnants of the pig, and there was an abundance of
beans, bread, cheese and wine to accompany it.

This was after the war and just before people were starting to leave for
Australia and Venezuela. Derì knew that for him that opportunity had
passed. He had his father's business to run and the wrong kind of wife
with whom to emigrate (blonde and frivolous). For a few years now he

had been married and trying to work steadily at the business his father had built up, and he was finding it difficult to accept his ordinary fate.

Derì often played the fool, which made grown men and women roll their eyes and sigh. While digging Bucchione's vineyard on the Leccio hillside with Gino and Sucker, he raced to beat the other two to the end of the row. During the wheat harvest he insisted on doing the most glamorous work, so he was the one to sit on the *moa*, driving the cows, as the sharp cutting blades and the movie cameras whirred.

At the Dinner of the Pig, Derì was again playing the fool. First he commandeered the ends of the bread loaves that Gemma had baked, sliced and piled into large baskets. The ends were everyone's favourite part of the loaf, and he pretended to spit on them to discourage anyone else from taking them.

Then he was still and silent for a while.

'Thwarted,' he cried out suddenly, rising to his feet. 'I have been thwarted. My life has been thwarted. My whole life is a thwarting of the most egregious kind.'

No-one knew in what sense he had been thwarted, let alone what 'egregious' meant, but they could sense that he was unhappy. They were shocked when he stood up and shouted the way he did and then sat down immediately, as if shot, and stared straight ahead with blank eyes.

He slowly came back to life and drank more wine. As he drank, he sang 'Signorinella', and occasionally someone would join in. Soon he was so drunk that the others were worried he would die. They had heard about this happening, and some had even witnessed it. The wine flowed so freely into the veins that instead of blood it was wine that fed the heart and the lungs and the brain. Derì drank so much that he was almost unconscious.

Bucchione, who was also very drunk, removed his battered blue hat, leapt onto the table and, demanding everyone's attention, exclaimed:

'Nobody need worry about a thing. I take full responsibility!' This struck the revellers as a ridiculous thing to say and caused general uproar. Several people jumped up beside him and bellowed into his face that it was a ridiculous statement and what did it mean exactly? Bucchione was adamant. He would be personally responsible for any disaster that might befall Derì. They all shouted him down and, over his protests, pulled him back into his chair and made him put his hat back on. The saying, 'Nobody need worry about a thing. I take full responsibility,' became a part of Villora folklore.

They left Derì to sleep in a corner.

In the small hours, after the carousing had died down, the silence of the village was shattered by the out-of-control screaming of a motorcycle engine and the sound of its wheels seeking traction on the icy road up near Clementina's house. No-one had noticed that Derì had left the party. When they rushed out they found him sprawled on the ground, bruised and grazed, bleeding and half-dead, with the bike nowhere to be seen. In fact, its engine was roaring and rear wheel spinning freely at the bottom of the ditch, under some bushes. Gino had to scramble down to turn it off.

Nedo, who had the only phone in the village in his shop, called the ambulance. As they waited, Derì started to sob hysterically and kept it up all the way to the hospital. He cried for three days.

He recovered well enough, although the light had gone from his eyes. The war ended. The years passed. His old father died. Life went on.

...

The man whose heart ruled his life was later betrayed by it. His coronary arteries became blocked; he had first a small heart attack, then a big heart attack, and died at the age of sixty-seven.

The Visitor

A few weeks before Derì died, his nephew Paolo spent a Sunday afternoon with him in the big white house. Derì was in a deep depression, partly because, Paolo suspected, depression ran in the family and partly because he had found out that his son, Giuseppe, named after the grandfather, was drowning in debt.

It is possible that there were two last straws in Derì's thwarted life.

His son had married an unsuitable woman whose family sold handbags at a stall in the marketplace. Children are born even of unsuitable marriages, and this marriage produced a little girl who went to live with her grandparents when the inappropriate wife left.

Derì and his blonde wife raised their granddaughter for five years until the mother returned to collect her. When the little girl was taken away, everyone heard Derì's heart crack like a bomb over Centoni. It echoed around San Ginese.

The second straw was a silent event. Two days after the granddaughter was removed from his life, his greatest friend, Bruno, who was the brother of his blonde wife, therefore his brother-in-law, died suddenly.

Derì and his wife were returning home after a visit to the new widow. As he inserted the key in the door of the big whitewashed house, Derì for the second and definitive time suffered sudden chest pain and discomfort, which travelled into his shoulder, arm, back, neck and jaw. He collapsed half in and half out, on the threshold. He died there and then.

Some years after Derì died, his son Giuseppe sold the house his grandfather had built and moved his mother, no longer a stunning blonde but still frivolous, into an apartment in San Leonardo.

The Dead Boy

They had named him after the Greek island home of Apollo, who was the Sun God and the Christ, and every day of his life was a Calvary and his fingers bled until he died and was the Dead Boy.

He was born and was a shy little boy, and every morning of his life he woke afraid of what the day would bring. The fear did not go away as he grew older. Even at the age of seventeen you could see it in the nervous tics around his blue eyes, in his squinting and blinking and his darting pupils that avoided looking straight at you. His hair was blond and curly and stiff like a wire brush. He parted it on one side or the other and sometimes, for a change, and to unsettle his mother, in the middle. He bit his fingernails to blood, and he stuttered so that his tongue sat flat behind his front teeth and froze while his lips moved up and down and his voicebox came in too late and he made *aahh* sounds and *eehh* sounds and other vowel sounds and then hit a consonant and went *t-t-t* or *gh-gh-gh*. And then he shut up. Maybe he was afraid because he stuttered or maybe he stuttered because he was afraid. It was only in order to overcome his fear that he was sometimes a rebel and behaved in a way that adults did not like.

He was a year younger than the Visitor and he never stuttered when they were together.

His father, whom everyone knew as Il Bianco for his fair hair, was called Gimi, one of those names that had been brought back from California. Il Bianco was a small tough chunk of a man, tanned to leather from working outdoors, handling bricks and mixing mortar, building houses. He lived all his life in a white singlet, regardless of the weather, and provided well for his family, but though controlled, he was an angry man, impatient with weak, ineffective people who could not build houses. Everyone could see the rage seething in him. On the other hand, Anna, the Dead Boy's mother, was a gentle, silent woman, who for protection from the world and perhaps from her husband always wore a headscarf. It made her look sweet and kind, so that you felt like letting her be your mother too. She was always asking you to stay for lunch or dinner, to be company for her friendless and frightened Dead Boy. Most of the time when she talked to the Visitor, she looked at the ground. The sides of the scarf were like a pair of blinkers on a horse and kept her from getting spooked.

The Visitor remembered the day he realised that he could easily have been like the Dead Boy. He'd been born in that village and could easily have stayed and grown up there and then he wouldn't have been who he was now. The thought of that possibility was overwhelming.

The Visitor was enrolled in the local high school but in an annexe away from the main school campus and away from the Dead Boy who, it was thought, would be a bad influence on him. As soon as they got home from school every day the corrupting of the Visitor resumed.

The Dead Boy was already thirteen years old when his mother gave birth to a baby brother. Mother and father had to have another one to make up for the mistake that the first had turned out to be. However, he loved his baby brother, who was weak, defenceless and needy like him.

...

The Visitor, who was trilingual, read, in the original language, Italian, French and American novels, including Alessandro Manzoni's *I promessi sposi*, Benjamin Constant's *Adolphe* and F. Scott Fitzgerald's *The Great Gatsby*, and would tell the Dead Boy about them. In return the Dead Boy, whose fear of the world seemed to disappear when talking to his friend about what his life would be like one day, would become excited and describe the lovers he would have one day, and occasionally he'd go, *eh? Eh?* and if his friend was close enough he would elbow him in the ribs.

Years later the Visitor wondered if his friendship had given the Dead Boy courage. He wondered whether in repatriating to Australia, which could not be helped, he had not forsaken the Dead Boy so that he lived in fear again. When he told him he was leaving, a strange stunned silence and a new distance was born between them. But while they were together, life was an adventure.

...

When they were older and could drive, they borrowed a car and went to Alfredo's at Colognora for pizza and beer. There the Dead Boy took control. First, they ordered a platter of sliced *salame* and prosciutto, olives, artichoke hearts in olive oil, with bread and *grissini*, breadsticks. They always drank foreign beers: Stella Artois, Tuborg, Elephant and Heineken, which went well with a mushroom pizza or a margherita with anchovies. The Dead Boy could turn an outing with a friend for pizza and beer into a party. Second, they just watched the girls.

Alfredo operated a roller-skating rink next to the pizzeria, but neither of the two boys was relaxed enough in their body to strap on skates and roll and roll with people watching, especially girls, and other boys rolling better than they ever could. Pizza and beer and watching the girls rolling was more than enough. It was perfect.

At Alfredo's there was a dance floor where bands played and young people like them jumped up and down to the music. The lyrics they sang were nonsense English, like *crastunoitainisi* – 'Christ, you know it ain't easy' from 'The Ballad of John and Yoko', which was popular at the time.

Not far from Alfredo's was an ancient cherry tree that belonged to the Visitor's paternal grandmother. The two boys sat in the tree talking about girls and eating cherries for two hours until they were both so sick they had to lie down in the grass and wait until the fruit had dissolved in their stomachs.

These were just some of the things they did. But most of the time they had nothing to do.

When the two boys became juvenile delinquents it was the Dead Boy who led the way. Maybe he was bored or had read too many *Diabolik* comics. Meanwhile, the Visitor, a watcher by habit, watched, and if he liked the idea or had no strong objections, went along with his friend, whose excitement was infectious.

On the occasion of their first delinquency they stood at the crossroads at the top of the Speranza hill and threw stones at the lone streetlight. The Dead Boy was better at juvenile crime and hit the large incandescent bulb and it exploded and the top of the hill suddenly went dark and quiet. Both boys spun around in a complete circle, surveying the landscape, afraid that someone in a nearby house had heard the loud pop.

A few nights later they visited an empty house halfway up the Speranza, set back from the road behind high white walls. The Dead Boy had taken one of his father's diamond-tipped tile cutters and he scratched a circle in the glass of the rear door. When he tried to knock the glass through and it didn't work, he shattered it with a rock and they crawled in through the hole. There was nothing to take. They had better luck when they forced the canteen door at the trout farm and found thousands of sticks of chewing gum, which lasted for months.

They did it for the excitement, the warmth and the tingling in the skin, and the accelerated heartbeat.

They were riding the Dead Boy's Vespa back from Lucca, where they had seen Brigitte Bardot in *And God Created Woman* at the local film club, when they decided to break into Gan-Gan, a small pink villa near Villora surrounded by trees and bushes growing wild. The villagers said that the house was a weekend retreat for some Milanese people. The Visitor found a pole, leaned it against the upstairs balcony, and they climbed along it upside down, like action heroes in a Hollywood movie. There were several bedrooms, each with a bed that had been stripped down to a mattress covered with a loose dust cover. The wardrobes were full of clean sheets and blankets.

In the refrigerator they found a large plaster penis. This seemed to confirm the gossip in the village that women were brought to the house for sex, something you expected men from the city to do. They tried to guess what the penis was for, apart from symbolising what the Milanese did at Gan-Gan with their whores, a bit like the phalluses chiselled into the footpaths in Pompeii pointing in the direction of the nearest brothel. All the two of them could come up with was that it was the cast of the penis of one of the men and it was in the refrigerator to dry out and harden so he could show it off. It looked much too big and coarse to actually be used, but then the two boys had no experience of these things.

As the sun came up, they sat on the balcony in armchairs, resting their feet on the low wall, drinking the dregs of several bottles of brandy, whisky and vermouth they had found, watching the lights of Montecatini going out in the distance, blinded by the flashing sheets of sunlight reflected off the factory rooftops in Porcari, beyond the drained swamp.

This was the time when the Dead Boy said to his friend, *Listen*.

Though the monologue that follows is not real, it sums up a typical pattern of thought of the Dead Boy and is intended to give an insight into his emotional life.

Listen, he said, holding up a hand to catch his friend's attention. *Listen*.

Imagine this woman, look at her: brown eyes, blue eyes – doesn't matter what colour her eyes are – eyelashes, eyebrows, cheekbones, the line of her jaw, lips, luscious lips, earlobes, earrings that say, look at my neck, the line of my neck, see the hollow above my collarbone, the wisps of hair falling down the side of my face, past my temples . . . what do you think about when you look at her? You look at her and you feel like you've just won a billion lire and all your problems are gone. She makes you feel like you could conquer the world. You're in an American movie, her movie and yours, you're both in it. You're driving a white convertible with the top down, a sportscar along the coast road towards Monte Carlo. You have both just had a bath – not a shower, a bath – and are wearing comfortable, loose but elegant casual clothes. You, a white shirt that fits beautifully, with three buttons undone, white slacks and white canvas shoes. Her, a dress to just above the knees, a cotton dress with a subtle floral motif that gently clings to her body sometimes, attaching itself just for a moment to a hip, or a shoulderblade or a breast, revealing the curve each time. You stop for a light lunch, grilled fish and a green salad, accompanied by a glass of white wine. Then you stroll along the beach arm in arm, and here a delicate breeze touches the fine hairs on her arms and on your arms. It's just a bit warm, and fresh enough too: the temperature is perfect. Strands of her hair float delicately around her mouth and you reach over and gently remove one that is resting on her lips and then you decide to take a room at the hotel where you just had lunch and you lie down on the bed side by side holding her wonderful rich fingers that take your breath away and you both fall asleep, her left arm resting against the entire length of your right arm, her breath on your face so sweet you want to eat it but can only breathe it in, and you both wake perfectly rested that evening, shower, change and sit on the balcony overlooking Avenue Princesse Grace and the water, the temperature again a perfect 20 degrees centigrade and she is there, extraordinary, and she smiles and the soundtrack plays and you don't ever want her to open her mouth and speak and certainly never to become the mother of your children or anything like that!

...

The Dead Boy keeps a large collection of Danish pornography in the attic of his family home and one day he shows his friend, who is surprised that things like that exist – women with dogs and women with penises, as well as the usual girls with large breasts. They sit there on the floor, next to an old wooden box, flipping pages and browsing through magazines with faded covers and pictures of naked women with lurid skin tones.

One night, the kind of night when wolves go roaming about, the Dead Boy announces they are going to borrow Romano Ragghianti's motorcycle. He asks the Visitor to stand at the bend in the road at Il Sasso, near the bar, and keep watch in case someone comes out and walks towards them, or in the event that a car arrives and turns into Beàno. The Visitor leans against the wall of Beppino's house with his hands in his pockets, stares at the sky and counts stars while scanning the road in all directions, and nods that it's okay. His friend forces open the door of the old stable and together they roll the new Moto Guzzi silently down the hill past Lida's place, then push-start it.

With the Visitor riding pillion they enter the freeway at Carraia and ride as far as the outskirts of Pisa in driving rain. The night is a blur of cars and trucks, water splashing, freeway lights, traffic signs, glossy bitumen and white lines. The rain stings their foreheads and eyes and ears, cold air burns their throats and tears at their lungs, and they are frozen and wet but so exhilarated they will never forget. They return the bike early in the morning, turning the motor off down near Sucker's place and, wheeling it up the slight rise into the village, stopping near Julio's stable to piss at the stars. No-one ever knows about Romano's motorbike. Even now there are only two people who do. This is one of those moments that enrich a life immeasurably, even when it becomes a memory, one of those moments that make a life worth being born into.

The boys play Monopoly in the attic of the old house where Morena was born and where Bucchione stored sacks of corn and his own old motorbike. Every time the Visitor climbs the stairs he sees the light patch on the wall where Gemma spread fresh plaster over the hammer and sickle on the night the blackshirts visited. In an old trunk there are letters that Morena received from Ugo when Ugo went to Australia by himself, before she and her son went too. The two boys have draped a tablecloth over the trunk and placed the Monopoly board on top. It's good when the Dead Boy wins at Monopoly, but sometimes the Visitor gets carried away, and having obtained a small advantage in his real estate dealings, presses it home, reduces his opponent to nothing and feels disloyal later, and it's bad for his friend the Dead Boy who again has not won.

The Visitor

There is another betrayal when the Visitor's life takes a turn for the better. He leaves San Ginese for a summer holiday in England and France and meets a girl who writes to him every week, and he goes to visit her, makes long overnight train journeys across Europe, while the sad boy with the frizzy hair and the stutter knocks and knocks at his door to ask him out for pizza and beer.

When the time comes for the Visitor to return to Australia, the Dead Boy drives him to the station in Lucca to catch the train for Rome. It is the last time the Visitor sees him. Over the years there is only an occasional postcard, from Lucca, Milan and South Africa, and once or twice a letter.

...

Despite his fear of being alive the Dead Boy has a girlfriend. The Visitor, who has returned to Australia and hears about it later, is told she isn't very pretty but, they say, with the Dead Boy's problems, what could you expect? As oral assessments are the standard form of assessment, and because his tongue is set in concrete, which makes talking to examiners a torture, the Dead Boy doesn't finish high school. He becomes a migrant, like so many others in San Ginese. He moves to Milan, works as a labourer on building sites and starts a small building-maintenance business.

...

Twenty years after they bury him, he's watching from a corner of the room when the Visitor visits Gimi and his gentle wife, Anna. The three of them sit at the table in the dining room and the Dead Boy senses his mother and father are wondering what on earth the stranger is doing there. They hardly know the man.

The Visitor sits there and either weeps or is on the verge of weeping in front of the woman who used to ask him to stay to eat and who still wears a headscarf, and the angry leather man who is still tanned but no longer builds houses and is now on a pension. The Dead Boy knows the weeping or imminent weeping confuses his parents. The Visitor tries to explain that their son was another one of those people whom he'd known once, for a short while, and who has died before he had a chance to say goodbye, and that the cemetery is now full of people like that. The old couple say nothing and wait for him to finish and go away.

...

For the ceramic photograph on his headstone in the San Ginese cemetery (the New Cemetery, not the Newest), the Dead Boy's mother and father have chosen a picture of him wearing taupe trousers, a floral shirt and dark glasses while holding a cigarette in a limp-wristed hand. The Dead Boy is looking past the Visitor towards something.

An Anagraphical Desire

There are times when ancestral curiosity, which most people experience at least once in their lives, is suddenly of the greatest importance and there is an urgency for you to know where you come from, possibly to discover where you are going. The Visitor recalls that a rush of ancestral passion once overcame Ugo and Ugo's older brother, Sucker, and transported them into a mental state in which they tasted, through the possibility of belonging to the past, if not immortality, then a beginning without end.

During one of Ugo's visits to Italy, the brothers spent an entire week searching through seventeen large registers and piles of loose parchment deep in the bowels of the church at Castello for a date, a name, a birth certificate, a baptismal certificate, a first communion certificate, a confirmation certificate, a marriage certificate, a death certificate – any anagraphical information at all about the ancestors of their great-grandfather Genesius.

In the course of their investigation they ate a bag of subterranean bibliothecarial dust (a *sacca*, as Gemma used to say), coughed up a thick brown pulmonary stew, stripped the meninges from their brains, which were clamped in the vice of cerebral trituration caused by the attempted decipherment of faded, written hands, and lost their way in ancient calligraphy and had to be rescued from the stupor into which they slid by their wives, who were called in by the priest when Ugo and Sucker stopped responding to the anxious cries the man of God launched through the open trapdoor, dispatching his oral missives down the twenty-seven flights of stairs once every daylight hour.

The two men had turned pages day and night by the light of fifteen candles and thirty-three paraffin lamps, not stopping to eat or sleep, but found no-one who preceded Genesius. They came to the conclusion that Genesius was the first and that those who came to San Ginesè before Genesius must have been *piovuti*, people who had fallen like rain from the sky.

When Ugo and Sucker came to the surface and staggered through the nave and into the courtyard of the church, they discovered half the village had gathered to greet them, fools who had been lost and now were found. As their anxious women hovered over them with urns of water, jugs of cloudy white wine, sheep's milk cheese, slices of polenta wrapped in pieces of coarse linen and bowls of white beans in tomato, they looked around and marvelled at the breathtaking beauty of the scene before them.

When the onlookers asked them who had come before Genesius, the two brothers, responding in unison, intoned, as if stunned: 'Nimmo. No-one.'

The crowd outside the church slowly dissolved, and everyone reluctantly returned to their fields and stables. Ugo and Sucker walked home, to the house of Genesius, which had become Tista's house and was now Vitale's house, accompanied by their wives, who held them by the arms for fear their men would topple over after their ordeal.

La Storia di San Ginese

If the Visitor were to be so inclined and if he were at a loose end on the third night, having walked around San Ginese three times the day before and dined in the small pink house where his mother was born, he would read a monograph by Salvatore Andreucci with the title *S. Stefano di Villora: the now vanished ancient Pieve of the Compito district*.

The Visitor would learn the following about the history of San Ginese.

A *pieve* was a major church, one which had a baptistery. Nearby churches without a baptistery answered to it. In the early Christian Church a separate baptistery building was necessary, as an uninitiated (unbaptised) person could not enter the church proper. So the unbaptised person was first baptised in the baptistery and was then immediately introduced to God, who was waiting in the adjacent building.

The Pieve di Santo Stefano was where San Ginese is now and existed in its primitive form already in the second half of the fourth century or at the latest since the fifth century. It was named after Santo Stefano, the *protomartyr*, meaning he was the first Christian martyr in the district.

The first ancient text in which Santo Stefano is called a *pieve* dates from Anno Domini 983. The naming occurs in a deed of donation, by which means Bishop Teudigrimo grants to Sisemundo, son of the late Chunerado, from whom are descended the Nobles of Montemagno, the entire estate of Santo Stefano with its major church and baptistery. (Note that in English the above names would be rendered respectively as Theudigrimus, Sigismund and Conrad.)

For the interested reader, what follows is the full deed of donation in Latin. It is given here in the original in the hope that it will afford an enhanced experience to those fortunate enough to be familiar with the language. It is published by Barsocchi in *Memorie e documenti per servire all'Istoria di Lucca*, vol. V, 3, doc. MDLXI (3), Lucca, 1841. The uninterested reader may ignore this section.

SALVATORE ANDREUCCI

S. Stefano di Villora:
la primitiva Pieve del Compitese oggi scomparsa

Estratto dal GIORNALE STORICO DELLA LUNIGIANA
Nuova Serie - Anno XV - N. 1-3 - Gennaio-Settembre 1964

ISTITUTO INTERNAZIONALE DI STUDI LIGURI
BORDIGHERA 1965

The Visitor

In nomine Sancte et individue Trinitatis. Otto grazia Dei
imperatore augusto, filio bone memorie itemque Ottoni
imperatoris anno imperii eius sextodecimo, septimo idus
augusti, inditione undecima. Manifestu sum ego Sisemundo
filio bone memorie Chuneradi, qui Chunitio vocabatur,
quia tu Teudigrimus gratia Dei et cet. per cartula livellaria
nomine et cet. idest omnibus casis et rebus seu terris
tam domnicatis quam et massariciis, cum fundamentis,
et omnem edificiis vel universis fabricis suis, que sunt
pertinentibus Ecclesie plebis vestre Sancti Stephani et S.
Johannis Baptiste, quod est plebem sita loco et finibus Villa,
quam plebem ipsam esse videtur de subregimine et potestate
et cet. Episcopo vestro Sancti Martini. Casis vero ipsis tam
domnicatis quam et massariciis cum fundamentis seu
curtis ortis ulivis silvis et cet. omnia et ex omnibus rebus
tam domnicatis quam et cet. quantas ubique et cet. ad
suprascripta Sanctam plebem sunt pertinentibus in integrum
mihi eas et cet. livellario nomine dedisti mihi, idest omnem
retditum edibitionem illam quantas singulis hominibus qui
sunt abitantibus in villis, qui dicitur Paganico, Colugnola,
Colline, Vinelia, Cerpeto, Vivaio, Colle, Tillio, Cumpito,
Vico qui dicitur ad Sanctum Augustinum, Faeto, Massa
Macinaria, singulis quibusque anni ipsius Ecclesie plebis
vestre Sancti Stephani et S. Johannis Baptiste consuetudi sunt
aut fuerint ad retdendum, tam de vino, quam et de labore
simulque de bestiis, aut de qualibet frugibus terre vel qualibet
mobilia. Iam dictum retditum seu debitum edibitionem,
quantas singulis hominibus qui sunt abitantibus in prefatis
villis, aut in antea et cet. singulis quibusque annis ipsius
Ecclesie plebis vestre, seu titulis et cappellis cum omni

eorum pertinentiis et adiacentiis subiectis ipsius Ecclesie
plebis vestre consuetudi et cet. in integrum mihi eas
livellario nomine dedisti. Tali ordinem ut da admodum
in mea qui supra Sisemundo vel de meis heredibus sint
et cet. suprascriptis casis et rebus seu terris domnicatis et
massariciis, quas nobis dedisti, eas abendi et cet. et nobis eas
privato nomine usufructuandi; et iam dictum retditum seu
debitum quas nobis dedisti, requirendi et recoliendi, et nobis
eas privato nomine habendi et usufructuandi, et faciendi
exinde quiequid nobis autilitas fuerit. Nisi tantum et cet.
exinde tibi vel ad posterisque et cet. ad pars suprascripte
Ecclesie plebis per singulos annos per omne mense magio,
censum vobis retdere debeamus ad suprascripta Eccl. domum
Episcopo vestro S. Martini, per nos et cet. vobis vel et cet.
argentum solidos viginti de bonos danarios…

Petrum notarium domini imperatoris scribere
rogavimus. Actum Luca.
*Ego Sisemundo in unc libello a me facto subscripsi.
*Ego Johannes notarius domini imperatoris rogatus
 teste subscripsi.
*Witternus notarius domini imperatoris rogatus teste subscripsi.
*Petrus notarius domini imperatoris post traditam
 rogatus subscripsi.

…

Put simply, the Latin document describes the estate that is to be
donated by the bishop. The landholding includes, as you are able to
see, the parishes dependent on the major church of Santo Stefano,
these being Paganico, Colugnola, Colline, Vinelia, Cerpeto, Vivaiuo,

218

Colle, Tillio, Cumpito, Vico qui dicitur ad Sanctum Augustineum, Faeto and Massa Macinaria.

Several names have persisted until modern times – for example, Colugnola (now Colognora) is where Alfredo makes pizzas. Colline (Collina) is where the Adulteress came from. Colle is where Irmo the Younger lives, whose birth precipitated Ugo's migration. Cumpito (Compito) is where the Enchanted Glade was. Tillio is no longer a place name but is the name of a major road, via di Tiglio.

Before Anno Domini 1000, the northern part of the low-lying basin was not covered by the waters of the lake, which in later years, during periodic inundations, lapped against the edges of the nearby towns. The lake later grew very large and brooding.

Until Anno Domini 1100, the conditions of life in the area must still have been good, if in a document from 1026 S. Stefano di Villora is referred to as the *Pieve in loco Lignola prope plebem S. Stephani que dicitur Villula (1), doc. 114*. It was certainly between 1050 and 1100 that the waters invaded the northern part of the plain and San Ginese began to decay, continually threatened by the flooding of the River Anser. The population was forced to abandon the places threatened by the waters and move to higher ground.

In a contract dated Anno Domini 1150, for the first time it is referred to no longer as a *pieve* but as Ecclesia de Villore – just a church.

The major church of Santo Stefano had lost its status. The waters had grown too close, the mosquitoes had bred in larger numbers and a significant part of the population had fled.

From another document that speaks of the 1680 pastoral visit by the bishop of Lucca to the 'parish church of S. Stefano the protomartyr', we are able to understand in what state of decay and abandonment the ancient church found itself, having lost its status as a major church some five hundred years earlier.

Reproduced here in full is the English translation of the afore-mentioned bishop's original document written in Italian:

> Having found the seal of the Altar Stone broken, and as
> well the stone itself from one end to the other, and having
> found that the altar was without any sacred furnishings
> at all, we declared the church suspended until such time
> as it is not equipped with a new altar stone with two
> candelabras, a cross, three tablecloths for the meals of the
> *S. Convito e dell'ultimo Evangelio*, an antependium and
> baldachin and all that is required, and until such time as
> it is restored to a state that is decent and appropriate for
> celebration; in the meantime such needs as there are for the
> mass shall be met at the nearest church; we allow time of
> two months for the above measures to be put in place under
> penalty of 25 *scudi*. In two months the cemetery shall be
> encircled by a hedge so that animals cannot enter there, and
> a cross is to be placed there under penalty of 6 *scudi*. In one
> month the internal part of the church is to be whitewashed
> and the roof is to be repaired where necessary, so that water
> cannot enter, under penalty of 4 *scudi*.

At the time of the pastoral visit of Bishop of Lucca Filippo Sardi in 1791 it is still a church, but on the subsequent visit in 1803, again by Filippo Sardi, Santo Stefano's fate is sealed. His report reads as follows: 'S. Stefano di Villora, previously under the patronage of the House of the Altogradi, having been declared an abandoned church, no longer exists.'

San Ginese lost its original major church, then its ordinary church, both in the hamlet of Villora. Now there is only the ordinary church at Castello, at the top of the hill.

The Visitor

San Ginese is so old and was once so grand that it is impossible to comprehend unless you stop and are silent, empty your mind of day-to-day affairs and allow the antiquity and the grandeur to surface, because if you were born there it is inside you somewhere.

The Moral of a Modest Tour of San Ginese

Having read the history, or the story – the word in Italian is the same – of San Ginese on the third night, over the next two weeks the Visitor would reflect deeply and at length on the meaning of what he has learned. Before leaving he might return to sit on the low wall in front of Paolo's house, opposite the house where Giorgia the whore once lived.

If the Visitor were to look around, he would see that the courtyard is almost empty. Some people now say there is no-one left in the village, have said it in fact for many years, but what they mean is that none of the original inhabitants are left. The only people left are those who fall from the sky like raindrops, *piovuti*. The people from outside are filling the empty spaces.

Already an Albanian family of eight has arrived and is restoring the old house that once belonged to the village drunk. The Albanian family consists of two grandparents, two parents and four children.

The courtyard is almost empty because the inhabitants of the houses, who are all retired pensioners, prefer to stay inside. There are no children inside, however, except for the Albanian children. And no children outside, except, this afternoon, for a small Moroccan boy on a bicycle. So the courtyard is only almost empty.

When he asks, the Visitor would be told that the boy is called Isa, and that the name of the boy's father is Giuseppe and his mother is called Maria. Isa, Giuseppe and Maria. Isa, Joseph and Mary. They are Moroccan, possibly, but then it is impossible to know as although they are referred to as Marocchini, all migrants from Africa are referred to as Marocchini, which literally means Moroccan. It is like the practice of calling anyone who has been to Australia an *americano*.

The Visitor leaves San Ginese and misses his flight to Melbourne after a fatal accident on the freeway to Rome airport holds up traffic for an hour. He is forced to book another flight for the evening. As he sits in the lounge of the Hilton Hotel at the airport awaiting his flight, he reflects on four memorable truths he discovered while sitting on Paolo's wall, four truths that he is unable to convey elegantly in words.

The first truth: Villagers once gathered in the courtyard on long summer evenings to tell stories and laugh, tease the overly sensitive, argue and fight, fondle and pinch buttocks in the dark. During the day in the courtyard, men and women went about their agricultural business, cows harnessed to carts, corn spread out to dry in the sun. They swept, they shouted at neighbours a few doors away, they stopped to talk, they threw brooms at children, sat on a chair in the sun to rest, invited one another inside. In winter they gossiped by one another's fireplaces with a cup of coffee or a glass of wine. At any time of year, if visitors arrived at dinnertime, they were required to eat and drink. Everyone always saw everyone else coming and going, in and out of their houses. They heard doors opening, creaking, slamming, windows opening and shutting, raised voices and loud whispers. The next day they would interrogate one another about late-night arrivals and departures. Heads protruded from upstairs windows, faces appeared at windows and behind curtains. At night there was usually silence, faint yellow light seeping under front doors and through wooden shutters, past the edge of a curtain.

The second truth: A family of eight Albanians is renovating an old house in San Ginese. Three generations of Albanians are hammering, plastering, laying tiles, plumbing, sanding, polishing, rendering, painting a house in an ancient village in Tuscany.

The third truth: San Ginese died in Anno Domini 1100 and was born again. The church fell into disrepair, the people fled the waters of the swamp. Then the people returned and prospered for a while. San Ginese is like the lizard of Roman mythology, that dies in winter and is reborn in summer.

The fourth and most significant truth: There is a small Moroccan boy riding a bicycle in the empty courtyard. He rides around and around and around.

HUMAN SACRIFICE

'A Luciana

Tommaso G. was from a town called Morrone del Sannio in the province of Campobasso, which is in the Molise region. Morrone del Sannio borders on the municipality of Lupara, the name of which suggests a relationship with wolves and is also the Italian name given to a sawn-off shotgun, but neither of these facts is of any significance to this story. What is of some relevance is that in the Morrone del Sannio district an ancient tradition of human sacrifice to the gods was replaced a long time ago by the compulsory practice of youths, upon reaching the age of twenty years, abandoning their home and going in search of new lands. This is what Tommaso G. did.

He left Morrone del Sannio in 1957 and sailed to Port Kembla in Australia.

At the same time as Tommaso G. left Morrone del Sannio, Ugo departed from San Ginese on an icy January morning and, after passing through Melbourne and Mildura, where he stopped for the grape harvest, also arrived in Port Kembla.

Port Kembla in those days was an important steel town, and the town's big steel company gave work to twenty thousand men. It was said that at any single time three hundred workers were leaving and another three hundred were being employed to replace them. Ugo quickly found work.

On the first day, when he arrived in the steel town, he asked at a café for directions to the Italian boarding house and discovered it easily enough. There was a vacant room and he took it. Tommaso G. was already there, obsessively singing, humming and whistling a song in the Neapolitan dialect, which was unusual because he wasn't Neapolitan. It was a sentimental song, popular in Italy at the time, although Ugo had never heard it in San Ginese, where he had not developed an interest in the wireless.

Ugo and Tommaso decided they would share shopping for groceries. Tommaso would cook and they would eat together. There were many times when Ugo was overwhelmed by sadness. He missed his wife and baby son, who were back in Villora, and he was grateful for Tommaso's company and home cooking.

They did not have a tablecloth to spread out over their small kitchen table, so Ugo laid out old newspapers instead. He set the table while Tommaso prepared the evening meal.

Tommaso's specialty was a spicy and aromatic tomato *sughetto*, which he stirred into a large pot of drained spaghetti that rested on a newspaper tablecloth in the kitchen of the Italian boarding house in the town of Port Kembla, in the state of New South Wales, in Australia, in 1957.

...

You have to believe – better still, imagine – that Tommaso is singing now as he cooks the evening meal. He is cooking and singing at the same time. Or, as has just been explained, is humming or whistling the song, in the kitchen of the Italian boarding house in the town of Port Kembla, in the state of New South Wales, in Australia, in 1957.

The song he sings is ''A Luciana'.

The song he sings is about a young woman from the Santa Lucia district of Naples. She wears a red shawl and a comb in her hair. It is interesting that in the song she remains nameless and is simply referred to as 'the woman from Santa Lucia'. Men lose their minds whenever she passes by. But this young woman is determined to safeguard her honour and is very difficult to approach. Besides, her father and brother keep a watchful eye on her, and her uncle is a local organised-crime chieftain and is also very protective. Despite all these obstacles there is a young man who desires her. He describes his condition as one of being cooked slowly. When he sees her strolling by it is enough to make him suffer the tortures of hell for a week. And all he wants, or so he says, is to remove her hair comb and let her hair fall down over the shawl and around her shoulders. Or so he says. So Tommaso is cooking the evening meal and himself is being cooked slowly. And he's singing the refrain '*lo scialle russo e pettinesse*'.

Tommaso sings in the bath and in the kitchen and Ugo listens, and sixty years later as he dozes in his son's lounge-room in north-east Victoria, enjoying the sun that streams in through the French windows, he remembers only the words of the refrain: '*lo scialle russo e pettinesse*', the red shawl and the hair comb.

...

While Ugo was missing his baby boy and wife Morena (who is now buried in the cemetery of a small town in north-east Victoria), Tommaso, who had some money saved, was dealing with the Australian authorities so he could bring his betrothed Luciana to Australia. Not only is her name Luciana but her name also describes a woman from the Santa Lucia district of Naples.

Tommaso probably saved Ugo's life during those few months they were together. Not only did he cheer Ugo up but he also fed him spaghetti with a rich, nutritious sauce at a time when Ugo was emotionally exhausted and had lost his appetite. The shift work didn't suit Ugo and he always lamented, to his sons and to anyone who would listen, the difficult time he had in that period of his life. Shift work ruins the digestive system, causing stomach pain, fainting, high fever and death.

Ugo, who had never been out of San Ginese and was naïve and trusting, struck up a friendship with a Calabrian that Tommaso didn't like. Tommaso warned Ugo about this Calabrian. Ugo, not having had time to go to the bank, was carrying on him four hundred Australian pounds that he had earned picking grapes. Tommaso agreed to hold the money in safekeeping so that if the Calabrian looked among Ugo's belongings he would not find it there.

Returning home after the night shift one morning, Ugo found that the hinges on his suitcase had been forced. Other boarding-house residents had also had their belongings searched, and some had had money and precious items stolen. The Calabrian had vanished.

Tommaso, who had hidden the money safely, handed it back to Ugo.

...

One Sunday Tommaso and Ugo were relaxing with their boarding-house friends, kicking a round ball up and down the street, when Tommaso fell and dislocated his shoulder. He was in great pain but refused to see a doctor. He wanted to pretend that he had hurt himself at work to get some sick pay.

The next morning Ugo, with great difficulty, helped Tommaso get dressed. The pain from his shoulder had grown worse. They nevertheless both went to work. The men had been working in a pit, cleaning out moulds, which was risky work, and Ugo agreed to help Tommaso with his plan. When Tommaso gave the signal, Ugo cried out and the supervisor came running to where Tommaso was writhing on the ground, clutching his shoulder, as if he had fallen from the walkway to the pit.

They brought a stretcher and took him to the hospital. The plan succeeded and he was given paid leave for two months, plus some compensation.

After that he could only cook with his left hand as he had to wear a plaster cast that encased most of the right side of his upper body, yet the food he prepared was as delicious as ever.

Ugo left Port Kembla not long after and went to Red Cliffs, a town near Mildura in Victoria, to pick more grapes. Many years later he visited Tommaso once in Melbourne, but then they lost touch.

···

As for the young Luciana, Tommaso's betrothed, whom he was sponsoring to come to Australia: one week before she was due to leave for Australia she died of a heart attack. This was unexpected and rare in one so young.

The gods had betrayed Tommaso G. and had reinstated without warning the tradition of the human sacrifice of a young person. This was despite the fact that Tommaso G. had fulfilled his part of the bargain by leaving in search of new lands. If he thought that would spare him the suffering of a human sacrifice, he was clearly mistaken.

And Moses Spoke to God

He was a shy man called Moses with thick, sharp eyebrows and a son who was sick and an attractive wife who was boisterous and colourful and a daughter who resembled her mother. That the mother was the way she was, was God's mercy to help her live with the boy's sickness. God had no mercy on Moses.

They visited friends and took the boy with them, and their hosts gave them biscuits and coffee and grappa, and someone always said the boy should have a glass because it would be good for him. They talked about the towns in the north where they, where they all, came from and about the other people from there who had also moved here. The talk was always about what people were doing here, their houses, their work, whether they made good money, who was getting married, whose children were doing what. Then it would turn to what people were doing over there, their houses, their work, whether they made good money, who was getting married, whose children were doing what. I was from San Ginese, a small village in Tuscany, but I loved hearing the place names of the northern towns: Danta, Santo Stefano, Calalzo, Pieve, Padola, Dosoledo, Campolongo, Costalta, Auronzo. In those days they were all haunted by the places where they'd been born, all those people, young and magnificent men and women who had come here on ships. They believed they would find success, and they did, the way anyone who has food and shelter is successful.

Moses, a quiet, serious man who repaired roofs and gutters, had been here twenty years with his wife, who was a dressmaker and worked in a small room at the rear of the family home in Caulfield. The demand for her work was so great that she was obliged to stop cooking for the family. Moses, the lively daughter and the pale boy managed to prepare small meals at which she sometimes joined them. She was the wife but behaved as she would have liked her husband to. A secret battle had started the moment they met, testing each other's strengths and weaknesses. She had won, not because Moses was not strong but because he just wanted to work and care for his family and watch them be happy. The rest he left up to her. He also found it hard to become involved in daily affairs – conversations, discussions, decisions – because he was by nature a gentle, passive man, and hard of hearing. His big eyebrows would lift and he would squint and tilt his head and stare at you, as if by concentrating harder he could retrieve the words that had come out of your mouth and floated past him without going in. It was just easier to step back and have his wife manage their life. He was in his element on a roof, alone with his memories of the mountains and thoughts of his sick boy, for whom he would pray as he went about his work.

I remember the boy standing with his back to the gas heater in our front room and gasping gently for air, mouth almost shut and nostrils a little flared, his chest working, trying to hide it and joining in the conversation the little that he could. Moses, who was born a little tired, and was weary before his time, recognised himself in his son, and for this reason loved him more.

We had never understood how sick the boy was, so although we knew he had been admitted to hospital again, it was a shock when the news came that he had died over there. His mother was never happy and the family had gone back with faith in the national healthcare system at home and in the clean air the boy would breathe in the snow-covered Alps. 'If you don't like it here, you can always go back,' the Australians said.

The funeral would have been a bad one, especially for the father, although I say that knowing it would have been just as bad for the mother. I prefer not to think about it.

Time passed, but not much.

One very dark night in the Dolomites, under an overcast sky whose invisible clouds obscured the stars and the moon, Moses stood at the foot of the nearest mountain and spoke to God.

'God, you gave me youthful physical strength and courage at the beginning of my life, and you gave me hope that I took with me to another country. And then you didn't have mercy on me like you had on my wife, you didn't make me noisy and interesting and confident, with good hearing. Although she is a good wife and I have nothing to complain about. You gave me a wonderful daughter who is like her mother, strong and interesting. You gave me a sick boy who took my heart and held it in his wheezy chest, where its beat followed the pattern of his breathing. Whenever he didn't breathe my heart stopped until he started breathing again. So for all the years of his life he kept me alive by breathing.

'My wife and daughter are strong and are made for living and I am not any longer and maybe never was. I'm tired, God, and I want to see my boy. He stopped breathing and now my heart no longer knows how to beat. I want to see my boy.'

This all happened more than thirty years ago and has almost been forgotten. I hope God answered him from the top of the mountain. I hope God told him everything would be well.

The Migrant's Lament

There was poverty in San Ginese. Worse than that. Life there was a misery.

I'm old and my memory confuses me, but there are some things you can never forget.

When they came back they didn't often talk about their lives in Australia. Maybe just a word or two here and there. It was in the past, after all.

The Australians took our names away. They turned Giovanni into John, Giuseppe into Joe, Marta into Martha, Anna into Anne, Raffaele into Ralph, so that we lost another small piece of ourselves.

They couldn't make friends, not even with their neighbours. They were lonely. Maybe because they didn't have the language.

The language was a problem we could not overcome. Italians opened shops and we Italians shopped in the Italian shops. This was inevitable when you remembered, for example, the food we ate in the village and the food available in Australia.

They would write home saying there was a lot of work in Australia, but there is more to life than work. And anyway, it wasn't as easy as they said. Even the photographs they sent were misleading. They sent back photographs of themselves standing in front of a fancy car that belonged to someone else.

The lack of language meant we were lost. So many ways to get lost. Lose your language, lose your name, lose your village. Of course, we could always go back if we didn't like it.

All they knew was work, so all they did was work. The Australians thought they were stupid and laughed at them and their ridiculous customs behind their backs. The Australians mimicked their gestures and manner of speaking and told jokes about them.

After we'd been back a few years, all evidence of our adventure in Australia had disappeared. We lost our passports, misplaced our medical records, burnt our ship's tickets and the letters from the government through the local labour office. We made bonfires.

No wonder that the Wandering Jew, a plant named for a people who didn't have a home and whose life has often been a misery, is called *miseria* in Italian. When you leave your home, your life becomes a misery.

It was a life like an animal's. I wish I had never gone.

Many men considered themselves unfortunate and caught up in some kind of ancient tragedy. Their children did not recognise them when they came back, and ran to hide in their mothers' aprons. The men stood in the middle of the street and cried. Someone cried out: '*Sono sfortunato!*' For years the children were wary around their fathers.

Some of us made money, but it didn't make up for the other things we lost.

Some lost their health.

We came back to what we knew. What we knew was familiar and therefore became repetitious and boring. So, after we had resettled, in a manner, we found the ocean acted as a filter for the misery of Australia and we missed it.

Human Sacrifice

They returned because wives forced them, threatened them, lost interest in them and told them so in their letters. One man returned because he hadn't slept for five years.

I was neither fish nor fowl.

Others came back because Australia was too far away. As if, had Australia been just down the road, they would have stayed there. As for those who did not return, with the passing of time they couldn't remember why they had left. All they knew was that they wanted to be back where they came from. But it was too late.

From the ship sailing into Fremantle we saw the first Australian dawn. We could see Australia in the distance. A flat strip of land. Blue sky. A line of low clouds that looked like they were crushing the land.

The Translator's Tale

There can be no remembering if there has been no forgetting first. Living needs forgetting. The burden of remembering is too much.

He was twelve years old when they took him back to San Ginese, the village where he was born. The boy soon realised that there were things he had forgotten, so he talked to his mother to find out what they were. He discovered he had forgotten things he knew nothing about and that both the quantity and the quality of his forgetting was large.

He had forgotten all the people and all the places. He had forgotten the houses and the stables, the vineyards and the olive groves, the willow plantations and the fields, the roads and walking tracks between the villages, the drained swamp that became cultivated farmland, the long low hill to whose flanks the villages clung loosely. He had forgotten the names of places: Centoni, Montanari, Castello, Francesconi, Preti, Colognora, Pierini, Il Picchio, Cecchini, Marchetti, Lecci. He had forgotten Le Servette, the hairpin bends on the hill near Lecci, so steep he could not ride his bicycle up them. He had forgotten the church at the top of the hill, the same hill where the baronial mansion – il Maggiorello – stood, where his grandfather owned the best vineyard in San Ginese, where his father considered buying a piece of land to build a new family home. He was baptised in that church, and his godparents were Rodi, who died at fifty, and Pia, Rodi's wife. He had forgotten them. He had forgotten the old cemetery and the view from the church square of the wide plain stretching out below in the distance to the smokestacks of Porcari and beyond, with picture-postcard-pretty Montecatini on the side of the distant hills. He had forgotten Viareggio, the seaside resort where after his father left for Australia his mother took him in the summer of 1957 because salty sea air was a good disinfectant for a little boy's lungs. To help him remember at least this there were black-and-white photographs of a two-year-old boy holding a giant beach ball on the sand and posing beside Donald Duck. He had forgotten four great-grandparents, four grandparents, four uncles, one aunt and one hundred and twenty neighbours who had followed his progress for the first two years and four months of his life. He had forgotten the bed and the room where he was born and the stairs from the floor below street level in his father's house, which he had also more generally forgotten.

When he returned, people asked him if he really could not remember anything from before, and he would shake his head and sense their wonderment at so much forgetting. Being young, he was puzzled by their reaction but also genuinely interested, and he asked himself what there was to remember. The people in the village remembered him but he couldn't remember them. For a while this made him feel strong – he possessed an absence of remembering about which everyone asked and at which they marvelled. He was the centre of attention for his prodigious memory loss. They wanted something from him, and he could see the yearning for it in their eyes. It was his remembering that they longed for. They sought confirmation that their memories were real and did not know what to make of this forgetting, which they took almost as an insult. Remembering likes company, after all. He wondered whether one day he would remember all he had forgotten or if it would stay forgotten.

'*Ma davvero 'un ti riordi nulla?*' his grandfather asked. 'Don't you really remember anything? *Eh, eri piccolo.* You were little.'

The old man's voice would trail off and he would roll his tongue around to reposition the cigar in his toothless mouth. And his mother's aunt would ask, '*Ma 'un te lo riordi quando ...?* Don't you remember when ...?'

And she would describe a memorable event in his young life: his mother feeding him stewed pears as he stood at the high end of his grandfather's hay cart in the courtyard, and he fell and split open his forehead and needed stitches.

That day the doctor, who must have weighed one hundred and fifty kilograms, was called to tend to him, but the road up the hill was covered in ice and the tyres of the car were not gaining any traction. Five men ran over from the fields to offer assistance, but after much pushing and grunting had barely taken the car a further ten metres. They got the doctor out of the car so he could walk, but he started slipping on the ice and could make no progress. Finally, three of the men positioned themselves behind him and pushed while the other two tied a rope around his waist and pulled from the front. In this way he made it to the patient's bedside.

When the doctor was paid, the boy went about the village repeating to anyone who asked, '*Cento lire,*' feigning the same disgust his grandfather had displayed when handing over one hundred lire to Dottor Venturini.

His father told him this, but he had forgotten it all, so when asked if he remembered, he would shake his head and say, 'No.' He had forgotten all that there was to remember.

If they had sailed from Genoa just two months later, he might have remembered something of Villora, but instead his first memories were of 374 Rae Street in North Fitzroy and playing in the street and going to the corner shop to get milk – two months after leaving, after one month of a sea voyage and one month of living in Rae Street. So remembering was a question of two months. There is a razor's edge before which there is remembering and beyond which there is forgetting. Rae Street was as close as he ever came to remembering San Ginese.

The ship sailed from the ancient seaport of Genoa, gliding past the old lighthouse, on the third of March 1958, and there was nothing before then. It was his mother who took him away to Australia. She held him tight and tore him away from the people and places he loved and that he would soon forget. She staunched the bleeding of memories with her stories but bequeathed him a deep, slow-burning homesickness that brought an ache into his bones that never eased and the source of which he did not comprehend until he was old.

Dramatis Personae

The line of Ugo

Genesius (Ginese) Giovannoni (who married **Angelina**), great-grandfather of Ugo. Tista's house in the *Aia dei Mattei*, the Mattei Courtyard, was inherited by Vitale, who was the last of the male line to occupy it.

Giovan Battista ('Tista') **Giovannoni** (who married **Ancilla**), grandfather of Ugo. Giovan Battista did well enough in America to pay off the family's debts.

Vitale, father of Ugo, who married **Irma Del Prete**, mother of Ugo. Vitale made his fortune in America and lost it in the great economic disaster that struck the world.

Ugo, who married **Morena** and emigrated to Australia.

Sucker (of the Flat Thumb), hothead son, brother of Ugo. Married the Adulteress. Emigrated to Australia for three years and made enough money to build a house in San Ginese.

Lida, sister of Ugo, whose first-born died of diphtheria. She was then widowed and subsequently almost became a saint.

Irmo, brother of Ugo, the Young One, who was conceived when the war ended because Irma, who thought her time had passed, allowed Vitale an intimacy.

Gino Giovannoni, Ugo's cousin.

Alfonsina Dal Porto, Gino's wife, who wrote a long poem about her love for Gino, then cleaned and cleaned the house until she died.

Neva Giovannoni, their daughter, who never married.

The line of Morena

Paternal line
Giuseppe Giovannoni ('Nonnon'), wife unknown, paternal great-grandfather of Morena.

Paolino Giovannoni (who married **Teresa**), son of Giuseppe, paternal grandfather of Morena.

Giuseppe (known as 'Bucchione'), father of Morena, who married Iose the Flour-Eater, mother of Morena. Bucchione's family lived in Beàno, a pocket of Villora.

Morena, who married Ugo and emigrated to Australia.

Dramatis Personae

Paolo, who stayed in San Ginese.

Gemma, Bucchione's spinster sister, who raised his children and did the housework and was almost canonised as a saint.

Orsolina, who married and moved to Pieve San Paolo, to her husband's house, as was proper.

Maternal line

Giuseppe Dal Porto, Derì's father, Morena's maternal grandfather, who went to America twice and was successful.

Carolina, Derì's mother, Morena's maternal grandmother, who suffered an exploding vein.

Derì Dal Porto, Morena's uncle, whose heart literally broke.

Giuseppe Dal Porto (**Barba** because he had a beard), Derì's son, who sold handbags.

Other characters

(including some who are barely mentioned or don't appear at all)

Ginetta Giovannoni, Gino's daughter, who married.

Lucio Giovannoni, Gino's brother, who emigrated to California and married a fat woman who was too embarrassed to be seen by his Italian relatives. She refused to visit Italy and would not let him visit either.

He waited until she died, then visited every year for ten years, and then he died too.

Renato Catani, a bigamist opera singer who holidayed every year in San Ginese to 'take the grapes', the way people would 'take the waters'. The grape cure was popular with city dwellers who went to the country to eat nothing but grapes for a week. He toured Argentina with his small singing troupe and never came back. Spent the rest of his life on the verandah of his new wife's hacienda drinking Mendoza Malbec.

Beo, Bucchione's nervous, toothless friend, who had been to America. Pale and skinny like a worm (a *beo*), his real name was Vincenzo.

Bruna, of the plump buttocks, much admired by Beo.

Folaino, who lived in the house on the corner at Il Porto and subsisted comfortably on the money he stole from Tommaso.

Giorgia, the village prostitute.

Il Baroni, married to Ada. When away at the war he addressed his letters to Ada this way: *Ada, Sotto le case, vicino a Zabino, Villora* (Ada, Below the houses, near Zabino, Villora).

Il Bertuccelli, a shoemaker.

Il Chioccino, a chaplain with a small dog.

Il Pechini, a fascist acolyte who was bashed within an inch of his life after the war.

Dramatis Personae

Julio the Orphan, who wore thick glasses, a brown coat and emigrated to Argentina. On returning he adopted the Hispanic spelling of his given name.

Liduina and **Mariella**, two starving imbeciles, who lived next to Tommaso the Killer in *le case di sopra*.

Lilì, Bucchione's neighbour, a wise woman.

Lo Zena, Bucchione's neighbour, with whom he feuded for forty years. Played the mandolin and the accordion. Carpenter.

Nedo, bar owner, son of Nedo and grandson of Nedo (all bar owners are called Nedo).

Il Pallone, a cobbler.

Sandrino Cenci, from the neighbouring village of San Leonardo, who went to Australia and had much bad luck. Ancilla sold her house to Sandrino's father, who then sold it to Bucchione. Buried in the Kilmore cemetery, where plots were cheap. Family *sparpagliata*, scattered to the winds.

Santin, an anti-fascist who died from a bashing or from a bout of diarrhoea brought on by fear of bashing.

The Mute, a pilgrim who for several months was given food and shelter by Tista.

Tommaso the Killer, who lived across the road from Tista's house, in *le case di sopra*. He killed Folaino, who had stolen his money in California.

Zabino, who boiled meat to make broth and threw the meat away. During the war he learned to eat the meat.

Acknowledgements

My thanks to all the people who read my work and gave me advice. They say it takes a village.

In particular, big hugs to the Inklettes, meeting in the underground vault in Swanston Street: Andy Summons, Ailsa Wild, Honeytree Thomas, Merryon Ryall and Craig Madden.

Thank you too to Antoni Jach's masterclass participants, meeting in the beautiful boardroom at the Wheeler Centre: Emily Bitto, Jane Sullivan, Penni Russon, Elisa Evers, Rob Hely, Ellie Nielsen, Jacinta Halloran, Lyndel Caffrey, Mick McCoy, Rosalie Ham, Yvette Harvey, Sarah Schmidt, Lawrence McMahon, Jennifer Green, Leigh Redhead, Janine Mikosza, Clive Wansbrough, Patsy Poppenbeek, Anne Connor, Anne Myers, Susan Paterson, Evelyn Tsitas, Glen Thomson, Karen McKnight, Tiffany Plummer, Lyn Yeowart, Mark Baker, Stella Glorie, Jane Leonard, Nick Gadd, Enza Gandolfo, Toby McCorkell, Kathryn O'Connor, Sue Robertson, Pauline Luke, Deborah Wardle and Heather Gallagher.

At RMIT University thanks to Megan Rogers, Lisa Dethridge and Christine Balint. Also, Rachel Matthews, my very first writing teacher.

Most of the images contained in *The Fireflies of Autumn* were sourced from my own collection. I am grateful to the Ames Historical Society in Iowa for the photo of the Percheron (page 8), the National Archives at Atlanta for my grandfather Vitale Giovannoni's World War I draft registration card (page 9), the New York State Archives for the photo of a logging cabin (page 12), to John Bland/Wikimedia Commons for the image of a bucket (page 18), to Iynea/Shutterstock for the illustration of a pig (page 191), to the Italian Institute for the cover of Salvatore Andreucci's monograph (216), and to Wollongong City Libraries and the Illawarra Historical Society for the photo of Port Kembla (page 231).

Early versions of 'The Percheron', 'The Bones of Genesius', and 'The Fireflies of Autumn' were first published in *Southerly*. The words sung by Cosetta in 'The Enchanted Glade and the Babbling Brook' on the night of the dance are my translation of lyrics from the 1928 song '*Il tango delle capinere*' by Bixio-Cherubini. In 'The Dinner of the Pig', the words to the song Derì loves are my translation of lyrics from the 1931 song '*Signorinella*' by Bovio-Valente. '*La Storia di San Ginese*' draws on material from *Santo Stefano di Villora: la primitiva Pieve del Compitese oggi scomparsa*, a monograph by Salvatore Andreucci, published in 1964 by the Istituto Internazionale Di Studi Liguri, Centro Nino Lamboglia in Bordighera, Italy. I'm grateful to the Institute for supplying a copy of the monograph's cover (page 216). I also wish to acknowledge that 'The Migrant's Lament' was inspired by and adapted with permission from Archimede Fusillo's report for the Italian Services Institute of Australia on migrants who have returned to Italy, *The Future in Their Past*, published by the International Specialised Skills Institute in Melbourne in 2015.

My deep gratitude goes to everyone at Black Inc., especially Chris Feik, who said OK, I want to publish this book, and put up with me, and hammered the book into shape. Thank you to Dion Kagan, Julia

Carlomagno, Erin Sandiford and Kate Nash, to Mary Callahan for her beautiful cover design and to Tristan Main for his elegant text design and typesetting.

I am of course grateful to all the people of San Ginese, the real one and the other one, for being there every time I go back, whether in the cemetery or in the houses. It's time for another visit, if I can find the way there.

Never finally, and always first, my love and gratitude to Anna, Sim and Dan, the most valuable people in my life, without whom nothing is worth doing, for their support and just for being around and keeping me sane.

Moreno Giovannoni was born in San Ginese but grew up in a house on a hill, on a tobacco farm at Buffalo River in north-east Victoria. He is a freelance translator of long standing. His writing has been published in *Island*, *Southerly* and *The Saturday Age*, and his essays 'The Percheron' and 'A Short History of the Italian Language' were included in *The Best Australian Essays* in 2014 and 2017. Moreno was the inaugural winner of the Deborah Cass Prize in 2016. *The Fireflies of Autumn* is his first book.